BILL
AND THE
STING OF DEATH

Gary McPherson

Dedication

Thank you to my wife. Thank you for your support over the years, and your editing insights.

Thank you to Jeffery Harris. You are not only a friend, but a fan. You are a true brother in Christ and a great encourager.

Thank you to my book and e-book readers

Thank you to my website readers

Thank you to my audiobook listeners

CHAPTER 1

Bill stood looking out his window at the dark storm clouds. His fingertips tapped the top of his putter as he stared longingly at the practice green nestled between the executive buildings in the Ballantyne office complex. Sheets of rain poured from the skies. With a scowl, he slipped his putter back into his golf bag and returned to his desk. Inside the dark office, the glow of the computer screen reflected off his blue eyes.

He checked his sent messages to confirm his email to the home office in London went as expected. The file sat there with a local timestamp of nine am. It was now two pm, and his bosses in the U.K. would all be on their way home. Bill scowled. No new messages had arrived.

He leaned back in his chair and put his feet on his desk. He looked up at the ceiling, "Why?"

His feet hit the floor with a thud. Bill stood, walked back over to the window, and tapped mindlessly against the cold steel frame. Rain blew against the glass from a gust of wind. He turned towards the doorway, took two steps, and stopped himself. Bill returned to his desk and buried his head in his hands.

"Anything I can do?"

At the sound of his administrator, Bill looked up and shielded his eyes from a flood of fluorescent light.

He squinted and waved her over, "Carol, close the door and have a seat. I need some advice."

Without saying a word, Carol closed his door and glided along the floor in her four-inch stilettos. Bill admired her dark, firm legs. She had the physique of a runner. Her black eyes met his for a moment. He looked down at his desk.

She sat down and said, "You don't want my advice."

"Why?"

"I know this is about Lori."

His eyes widened. "Oh, you've heard?"

Carol gave a quick wave of her hand, "I'm your administrator. Nothing gets past me; that's my job."

Bill crossed his arms, "Alright, give it to me. What are you thinking?"

"I think you're a damn fool."

Bill rested his elbows on his desk and leaned closer to Carol, "I'm sorry, what?"

Carol leaned in towards Bill until their faces were inches from one another. "You heard me. What were you thinking? Dating a subordinate and then getting her knocked up?"

Bill flopped back in his chair, "It isn't like that. Besides, who said she's pregnant?"

"Please, women know these things. She's been glowing for weeks, and I don't mean because of her makeup."

Bill cleared his throat, "Who said it's my kid? I mean, assuming she's pregnant."

Carol let out a sarcastic laugh. "I'm sorry, Chief. I see how she looks at you. It's obvious."

"Does anyone else suspect?"

Carol shrugged, "Just the gossip crowd. I told them they should keep their thoughts to themselves, but you know how much good that does."

Bill nodded, stood, and started to pace.

He asked, "Have you heard from the home office today?"

"I have."

He walked over and leaned against the window pane. "If they went to you instead of me, it can't be good."

"I'm not sure what it is."

"Well, give it to me," responded Bill.

"I got a cryptic email saying they would be sending a man over to meet with you personally about personnel options."

Bill sighed and was quiet for a moment.

Carol said, "That doesn't mean you're fired."

"Oh, don't worry. I planned for this."

"Is that why you bought that little shack in Stallings?"

Bill answered, "It's hardly a shack. That real estate is in a prime location and a great investment. Besides, three bedrooms are plenty for a couple starting out."

Carol pointed at Bill's chair, "Have a seat."

Bill walked over and sat down.

Carol asked, "We're friends, right?"

"The closest of friends."

"Good. I need to talk to you as your friend."

"Go ahead."

Carol continued, "I don't like what Lori has done to you. First, you sell off your condo in uptown Charlotte."

Bill interrupted, "Uptown isn't what it used to be."

"Granted, but there's more. This sudden move to the suburbs among the working class instead of one of Ballantyne's nicer neighborhoods. I feel like she's lowering your bar, not raising it."

Bill cleared his throat. "It's like this. I assumed I could lose my job. When you tell your boss that you'll quit if they fire your fiancée, you don't really have a bargaining position. We wanted an inexpensive property we could afford and would do well when we sell it later."

Carol asked, "What will you do if they fire you?"

"I'm thinking of day trading. After all, I've made other people rich. Why not take my savings and help myself?"

Carol ran her finger down her partially exposed thigh. "I just feel like you could have done better."

Bill raised his eyebrows, "I never thought of you as the jealous type."

Carol's eyes grew wide, and her jawline tightened. "If I wanted you, I would already have you. I, for one, don't think you should sleep with your boss. At least, not as long as he is your boss."

Bill leaned back in his chair, quiet for a moment. "It wasn't like that. You make her sound cheap. I pursued her."

"Oh, so she was the most attractive woman in the office?" asked Carol sarcastically.

Bill stammered, "No, I mean, well, yes. I'm not sure. Look, you made it clear, hands-off."

Carol nodded a couple of times as she smiled. "I see. So, you were trawling for women at the job like the gossipers say."

Bill looked up at the ceiling, "Why?" He looked back at Carol, "Look, I've never had a family. Family means more than money or anything else to me."

"You're a successful investor. Women aren't a problem."

"I don't want women; I want a wife. I want someone who will be my partner, and maybe someday we'll have kids of our own and raise them together. I realize that sounds a little strange in this place, but you should try growing up as an orphan. Families are more valuable than gold."

Carol answered, "So, you couldn't go to church like every other single person and find yourself a decent spouse?"

Bill looked down, "What's wrong with Lori? Besides, I haven't been to church since I left the orphanage. God hasn't seemed interested in my life. I prayed for a family day and night. I believed God would give me one. Isn't that what they teach? Faith like a mustard seed or a little child. Well, I had that and more. Still, nobody ever adopted me. Adam, the administrator, said my birth mother wouldn't allow it, but if there was a God, it seemed to me that's a small detail. If he couldn't find me a family, how can he possibly find me a wife? No, the church isn't for me, thanks."

Carol stood, "Alright, family man. I don't know who the office is sending, but I wish you luck. Whether you stay or go, I'll always have your back, and we're friends forever."

Bill stood and quickly made his way around his desk. He gave Carol a long hug. Coconut and vanilla filled his nostrils, and before he could stop himself, he nestled his face into her neck. They stood for several seconds, and Carol finally pushed him back.

"Take it easy, family man. Your future wife may disapprove if she walks in."

Bill protested, "It's just a hug."

"I know, but you have to start thinking about what Lori sees when we're talking together."

Bill pushed his hands through his thick, black wavy hair. Carol opened the door. She gasped, staggered backward, and collapsed on the floor. Bill rushed to the doorway. A man dressed in black with a black ski mask shoved his rifle butt into Bill's diaphragm without saying a word. Bill fell to his knees, gasping.

His eyes blurred, and he attempted to lift his head and focus. Another man clad in black stood by Lori in her cubicle down the row from his office, and two more men appeared to be guarding the front entrance.

The stranger next to Lori spoke with a British accent, "Are you the bloke in charge?"

Bill's forearms tingled, and soon his entire body felt like he had stuck his finger in a light socket. Muscles tightened, and vibrated. His vision went black, and a bright light appeared.

An unseen voice whispered, "Protect the village."

The office came into view.

The assailant beside him hit Bill in the head with his rifle barrel and ordered, "Answer the man."

The sharp pain instantly turned into the most pleasurable feeling Bill had ever felt. Bill grabbed the rifle barrel and growled, "Do it again."

CHAPTER 2

"Let go," yelled the stranger.

Bill held tight to the rifle barrel.

The Brit pulled a pistol, grabbed Lori by the hair, and put the gun to her head. "He said, let it go."

Bill released it without saying a word. The Brit said something, but Bill could not hear him over his heartbeat, pounding in his ears. He cocked his head to the right. The Brit tapped his gun on Lori's head.

Bill growled, "Let her go."

"Oh, tough guy, eh? What's the matter, is she your pigeon?"

The stranger looked down at Lori's hand and noticed the diamond on her right ring finger. He let go of her hair, twisted her hand, and held it up. She let out a squeal.

Bill snarled, "You'd better not hurt her."

"Ah, smart bird, this one. I believe you Americans wear your engagement rings on the left."

He let go of Lori's hand. She cradled it to her chest.

Bill's muscles began to coil. He wanted one of the men to make a move, any move. He would kill them all before he was done. "Get out,"

"All in good time, guv'ner."

The Brit shoved Lori into her chair and tapped his palm with his pistol. "First, we're going to have a little talk."

Bill snarled, "What do you want?"

The stranger laughed, and his men joined in.

Bill clenched his fists.

"You need to relax. I have one simple question, where's Harold?"

The name seemed familiar, and for a moment, his muscles relaxed.

Bill asked, "What's his last name?"

The rifle barrel whacked him in the head again, and his muscles tightened. He could begin to see the veins in his retinas superimpose on his vision.

"Stop wasting my time," demanded the stranger. "You know full well who I'm talking about. Harold Brown."

Bill cocked his head to the left, "Parabolic Defense Systems?"

"The same."

Bill's lips twisted, "Why don't you call Forbes?"

Lori spoke up, "How would he know?"

The Brit turned his attention back to her. "Oh, I forgot about you, bird. I bet you know a lot about your boy's secrets. Let's play a little game. You tell me what you know, and I won't kill you."

"No," growled Bill.

"Relax," said the Brit. "This is a straightforward game. I'll even give your lovey here a few hints. You see, Harold is your fiancée's brother. My employer needs to meet with him most urgently. It's a matter of personal importance."

Bill spoke up, "I don't have any family."

The Brit replied, "I wish I could believe that. I might have believed you a few weeks ago. Joshua is the sort of man to hide such things, but the situation has changed. We know they're looking for you. We had a bit of a hard time finding you, what with you moving offices and residences, but here we are. I'm quite certain the government has already found you."

Lori interjected, "We don't know what you're talking about. I don't know who you are, but you have the wrong man."

"I don't think so," replied the stranger.

Bill gasped as he watched the pistol rise. The world turned red, and he reached for the gun barrel of the man beside him. He jerked the assailant to the ground with one fast move. He put his knee on the man's neck and yelled, "Stop."

The Brit's gun went off and everything slowed down. Bill watched Lori's head jerk to the side and her eyes become glassy. Bill's knee drove down into the man beneath him. He felt the spine pop and a smile spread across his own face. Before he could inhale his next breath, Bill was on his feet, and he pulled the dead conspirator into his office. He shut and locked the door.

Bullets came flying through the drywall, and Bill dropped on top of Carol. He could hear the Brit yelling for them to stop shooting. The room got eerily quiet. He sat up and reached for the rifle. Bill pressed a button behind the trigger, and the magazine dropped on the floor. He picked it up and wrestled it back inside the gun.

Bill could feel his breathing was starting to become more labored. Tears streamed down his cheeks. The rifle was heavy and Bill laid it across his lap.

From the other side of the wall, the Brit hollered, "Look, mate. You lost your dove, but you killed my best man. What do you say we start over?"

Bill focused on controlling his breathing. The room's colors were starting to penetrate past his red vision, and he could hear his heart beginning to slow.

The Brit hollered again, "You can't simply hide in there, and I'll go away. Hmm, who is the next person I see? Oh, how about this nameplate? Lisa. Bill, come out in two minutes or Lisa's next."

Bill hollered through the door, "Who's the coward? You're targeting the women."

"What is it you Yanks say? Women and children first."

Bill's breath became shorter, lighter. The rifle felt like a feather, and the room turned red.

"Don't be a bloody fool," begged the Brit.

Behind the door, Bill stood silent. Carol moaned and looked up at him. Bill put his finger to his lips. Carol remained still.

He could feel his breath on the back of his hand that held the rifle in front of him. He could hear footsteps coming towards the door and the Brit's muffled voice giving orders from Lori's cubicle. The footsteps stopped in front of the door.

A howl escaped from Bill's throat. The door reverberated, the windows behind him shook. His coffee mug vibrated across his desk. He heard Carol's voice in the distance as he put his shoulder into the door with all his might. Aluminum, steel, and wood splintered with a crash, a screech, and a crack.

Bill stomped on the man's throat that lay on the floor in front of him, covered in shrapnel from the door. He quickly raised his rifle and fired before the Brit could get his revolver level. One gut shot sent the man to the ground. Two hot rounds entered Bill's side and exited out the back. The burning flesh felt good, and he laughed before he could stop himself.

He turned to find the last assailant running for the door. Bill fired, and a bullet exited the man's head. The momentum brought his lifeless body to the floor face first.

The Brit laid moaning on the floor of Lori's cube. Bill mechanically walked towards the dying killer. He saw the love of his life ashen, her eyes staring into nothing, and pieces of her brain stuck to the metal bookshelf next to her.

The Brit pulled off his mask and winced as he begged, "Please, it wasn't supposed to happen this way. We were told you were peaceful, compliant. It was only a question."

Bill removed the rifle strap from his body, raised the stock over the Brits head, and brought it down with all his might. The skull cracked, and blood sprayed up against Bill. He hit him again and again. Soon, the face was not recognizable, and Bill started on his body. He could feel the ribs crumble beneath each strike. It felt good, right.

Carol's pleading, shaking voice could be heard behind him, "Bill, he's dead. Stop, this isn't you."

Bill stopped. Blood dripped from his nose and lips. His office shirt was soaked in the blood of his enemy. He looked around to find everyone staring in horror, except Carol. She slowly walked up, reached out with shaking hands, and took the rifle from him and gently place it on the floor.

Carol's lips trembled, and her voice was barely audible, "Come with me to your office, and let's get you cleaned up."

Bill took a step, but then the room started to move. The floor felt like it was rising first from the right and then the left. His legs felt like lead, and his lungs gasped for air. He collapsed on the ground and leaned against a cubicle wall. He tried to focus on his breathing.

Carol spoke up, "Everyone, get to your cubes and prepare to evacuate. I locked the office down from Bill's desk. The police and EMTs are on their way. Remain in your cubes until the police have released you."

Bill could hear the workers meandering to the cubicles, and hushed voices as the sound of laptops closing and laptop bags zipping filled the silence.

Carol came and sat down next to Bill with some paper towels. "Close your eyes. I need to get this blood off your face." She looked down at his shirt, "Is any of this blood yours?"

Bill shrugged and winced from the white-hot pain that seemed to appear from nowhere in his side.

The damp towel felt cold and refreshing as she cleaned up around his eyes, lips, and nose.

"You are one crazy man," she said. "You could've got yourself killed."

Bill sucked in a breath and answered, "I don't care. They killed Lori, and they were going to kill more. I had to do something."

Carol pointed over her shoulder at his office, "Did you see your door? How did you do that?"

"I don't know."

A pounding at the front door caught their attention.

Carol began to stand up, "I'll let the police in."

Bill grabbed her wrist. "No, I'm still the boss. I need to do this."

Carol helped Bill slowly stand up. He leaned against the walls and made his way to the door. Peering through the glass was a policeman in tactical gear. Bill held up one finger and then typed in the combination on the keypad. As soon as the magnetic lock clicked, the police stormed in. They threw Bill against the wall and handcuffed him.

From behind, he could hear Carol yell, "Not him, that's our boss, he saved us."

The policeman who handcuffed him asked, "What's your name?"

"Bill.."

Bill stopped speaking and tried not to throw up on the officer. The floor moved again, and the world started to disappear down a pear-shaped tunnel. Beads of sweat formed on his forehead.

The officer asked, "Can you hear me."

The tunnel became narrower, he could hear Carol sobbing, and then Bill tumbled into the darkness.

CHAPTER 3

"Bill, wake up."

Bill smiled at the sound of Lori's voice. He tried to open his eyes, but had to shield them from the sun's glare. Lori's familiar silhouette stepped in between him and the sunlight.

Bill stammered, "Wait, where am I? I don't understand."

Lori stooped down close to Bill. The smell of leather filled his nostrils. Lori's familiar shiny black hair and hazel eyes gazed at him, but her outfit was made of rawhide. A short sword hung at her waist, and an ax head peeked out over her shoulder. Lori's familiar toned, olive legs peered out from underneath her thick leather skirt.

"Are you okay?" she asked.

Bill felt a cool breeze on his chest. He looked at himself and realized his shirt was missing, and his pants were made from some sort of hand-tooled leather. A piece of fur hung at his waist. He felt up his back to the top of his head, and his hand landed on a set of teeth. He scrambled to his feet and tore off the fur. The face of a wolf stared up at him from the ground.

The wind chilled his back, and Lori put her gloved hand against his bare chest.

"What's wrong, honey?"

"Where are we?"

Lori slipped her arm around him and moved to his side. "Don't you recognize your own town? This is Helvsgud."

"Am I dreaming?"

"No. Did you hurt yourself when you fell off the longhouse roof this morning?"

Bill closed his eyes and tried to remember. The familiar stench from the pig farms made him feel at home.

Bill asked, "How long have I been sleeping?"

Lori hugged him with both arms and nestled her head against his chest. "Not long. Are you sure you're doing okay?"

Bill gave her a squeeze and then pushed her back. "Of course. Over there are the accursed pig farms that keep our little town wealthy. You should start to worry when I forget about those. Speaking of wealth, has my father returned from Britannia yet with this year's taxes?"

Lori shook her head.

"Very well. I suspect nothing less from my parents. I'm sure it will be worth the wait."

Bill gazed out over the wall at the flatlands that lay outside their protections. Lori placed the wolfskin back on his head, and he reached down to find his familiar battle axes at his side. In addition to the pig farms, the flatlands were a patchwork of grains for the village.

Lori asked, "Are you going to order the villagers inside the town before the raiders arrive?"

Bill rubbed his chin, "It could be minutes or days until they get here. We will devastate our own village by taking the farmers from their work without the raiders having to lift a finger. No, we'll call them in at the first sign of trouble.

"Please, go attend to the militia and make sure they are ready when the time comes. I'll remain up here."

Lori dipped her head and quickly descended a nearby ladder. Bill smiled as he admired her form. She disappeared between the thatched roof houses nestled close together. In a few moments, she reappeared in the clearing near the longhouse. He watched her head inside and return. She blew a horn, and the men and women of the town assemble before her.

Bill turned back toward the farms, and the woods, lost in thought. He spoke quietly to himself. "Is this a dream, or was that a dream? Both feel so real. I know who I am. I'm a soldier who was called by Oden to protect this town, but that other place. Those people, they needed me. And Lori.."

His train of thought was interrupted by the sound of the sentry's horn on the village wall's far corner. Bill blinked and realized smoke had begun rising from the farms, and the villagers were running towards the gates. Without hesitation, Bill slid down the ladder and bounded out of the gates towards the smoke. His battle-axes hung at his side.

In a few moments, he heard the creaking of the gates as they closed. Then they opened again, and Lori sprinted to his side.

"Where's the militia?"

Lori caught her breath, "They're still forming. Freja's in charge and will be here soon. Besides, the two of us can take on a band of raiders."

Bill grunted, "Only one of us has Oden's hand upon them."

"I can take care of myself."

Bill's gazed into her eyes. "I know you can."

The raiders soon appeared through the smoke and fire. They stopped at the sight of Bill.

The leader yelled out, "We have no fight with you, Berserker."

Bill answered, "This town is under my protection."

The leader did not move from his position but asked, "What is your name?"

"I am William, son of Oden and child of Helvsgud. What is your name?"

"Bobby."

Bill blinked and stood silent for a moment. "That's it? Just Bobby?"

"Yes." Answered the stranger.

Lori and Bill looked at each other, and Lori shrugged.

Bill turned his attention back to Bobby. "Leave now, and I won't take your life for burning the farms."

Bobby's laughter surprised Bill. He knew who he was facing. How could he be so cavalier?

"Did I say something amusing?" asked Bill.

Bobby quipped, "There are two of you, and fifty of us. Even for a Berserker, you don't stand a chance."

Bill thought about his position. If he was alone, his odds might be better, but Lori was an accomplished fighter and could hold her own. Still, he had to stall for the militia.

Bill hollered back at Bobby, "I won't surrender the town, but tell me what you want."

Bobby pointed towards the wall, "We want your pigs and the taxes from Britannia that have arrived."

Bill crossed his arms. "Friend, you have been misinformed. The taxes have not arrived, and we have not gotten word of anyone returning from Britannia anytime soon. I'm afraid you've arrived too early."

Lori laughed at the end of Bill's statement.

Bobby pointed at Lori, "Then I'll take the wench."

Bill dropped his arms, and his hands clenched the top of his battle axes. "You and I will both die before that happens."

The sound of the gate opening behind him caught Bill's attention. With a blow of the horn, the militia came pouring out of the town. Bill turned back to find Bobby and his men rushing towards them. He pulled out his axes and sprinted towards his prey.

The pounding of Bill's feet was soon replaced by his heartbeat. His vision grew more acute, and the world turned crimson. Bill pulled out one ax and threw it. Its blade landed in the skull of the fastest man. An arrow pierced his side. The shaft protruded from his stomach and back. The pain from the weapon brought a shiver of pleasure to Bill, and he howled and headed for the man who shot him.

He knocked two more men aside and yanked the young archer up by the throat. Bill reached behind with his free hand and pulled out the arrow, laughing as it exited. The terrified young archer watched in horror as Bill spun the shaft around. He buried it in the young man's chest. Bill released his grip, and the body fell to the ground. A blade attempted to bite through his wolfskin. Bill spun and grabbed the sword by the edge and snapped it. His fist connected with the raider's skull with a sickening sound of bones crunching. Bill took the broken blade and stuck it through the raider's throat.

A commotion caught his ear, and he turned to see what was going on. Raiders backed away, and men and women of the militia fell back towards the town walls. Between them, Bobby stood with a knife to Lori's neck.

He yelled, "Stay back. I'll kill this wench."

Bill walked towards Bobby undeterred. He growled, "Let her go."

Bobby pushed the blade harder, and a trickle of blood ran down Lori's neck. Bill's pace quickened.

Bobby yelled in a panicked voice, "Stop, or I'll kill her."

Bill's voice caused everyone but Bobby to fall back further, "Leave her, or I'll rip your throat out."

Bill stopped, reached down, and took a sword from a dead raider. "Leave her."

Bobby stammered, "Don't make me do it."

"Leave her."

Bobby's hand quivered, and the knife bit deeper. Blood began to pulse from Lori's neck. Bobby dropped the blade and started backing up with his hands in the air. Bill started running at him. It felt like an eternity to Bill before he reached Bobby. In his rage, Bill lifted Bobby off the ground by his neck. With a quick twist of the sword, Bill slit open Bobby's throat and yanked his spine out through the opening.

Pieces of Bobby's throat came flying out of his neck, and blood sprayed from the wound and covered Bill. Bill dropped the body. He turned and fell to his knees beside Lori. She lay in a pool of her blood, trying to speak. Bill howled in anguish, and everyone ran away.

Lori sputtered, "I love you."

Her eyes glazed over and then stared blankly at the clear sky. Storm clouds began to roll in, and the sun disappeared. Bill howled again and cried. The crimson world quickly dissipated. He gasped for air, and the heavens opened, and rain drenched his body. Lightning struck the ground around him again and again. He fell onto his hands and knees and then rolled over on his back. He hoped he would drown in the rain and join Lori. Nausea washed over his body, and then Helvsgud slowly disappeared.

CHAPTER 4

Bill's nose crinkled at the odor of bleach and antiseptic. He opened his eyes, and a bright light flooded his vision. He turned to the left and opened them again. A chrome guardrail lay next to him. His next breath brought a stabbing pain that dissipated as he quickly exhaled. Carol sat bent over against the railing. Her firm, dark hands held and caressed his as she prayed quietly.

Bill pulled his hand from her grasp. Carol sat up and wiped the tears from her eyes.

"You're awake."

Bill looked around the hospital room and answered, "Am I? I just had the most horrible nightmare, and now I'm back in this one."

Carol laid her hand on Bill's shoulder. "I'm sorry. I don't know what to do except pray for you."

"Save it. If there was a God, He would have saved Lori."

Carol answered, "That isn't how He works, and you know that. Please, don't push Him away when you're in so much pain."

Bill tried to raise his bed, and the pain in his side made him stop. "Speaking of pain, can you get a nurse in here. I'd love to get some pain killers. I can hardly breathe."

Carol was about to get up when a nurse walked in. "I see my patient is awake. Good. I bet you want some pain killers."

Bill replied, "You're good."

"I know my way around the hospital. My name's Denise, and I'll be taking care of you for the next ten hours. If you need anything, just let me know."

Bill grunted.

Carol asked, "What time do I need to leave."

"When Bill says it's time."

Bill started to say something, but pain shot through his muscles.

Denise put her finger up. "I'll be back in a minute. Try not to do any sit-ups while I'm gone."

Carol spoke to Bill, "I'll take care of things until you can get home."

Bill gasped, "What about Clark and Company?"

"Don't worry about them. The home office sent out a form email to the branch reminding everyone not to speak to the press. Of course, that was after several scared workers had been ambushed by reporters in the parking lot trying to leave after the shooting."

"Nobody mentioned my name, did they?"

Carol shook her head. "The cops were clear to keep your name out of the press because it could put you in danger."

Bill gave a shallow, quick nod. "Good."

Carol stood up and made her way to the opened door. She started to close it when Denise came back in with a medicine pack. Denise quickly made her way to Bill's bed, took a clean Styrofoam cup, poured some water into it, and stuck the pills and water in front of Bill's face.

"Take these. You'll be feeling good enough to move around, but the pills will make you sleepy. That's how I keep you acting like a good boy so those wounds can heal."

Bill swallowed the medicine, and Denise took his vitals and finally left the room. Carol closed the door behind her. She walked back to the bed and looked once over her shoulder before speaking to Bill.

"There's a woman in the waiting room. She's with the FBI. A Cindy somebody. I don't know who those guys were, but evidently, there's more going on than the shooting."

Bill stared up at the ceiling, waiting for his pain to improve. "Did she ask you anything?"

Carol sat back down and whispered, "Yea, weird stuff. She wanted to know if we were dating and had you ever mentioned any family members to me. Then she asked me about some guy named Chuck. I told her I'd never heard of him."

Bill's head was beginning to feel light, but he could move with only a dull pain in his side. He raised the bed, faced Carol, and said, "Chuck. Some guy named Chuck called one night when Lori was over. It was a long time ago when I still lived in the condo. I only remember because he wouldn't go away."

"What did he ask?"

"Something about my brother. I told him I didn't have one."

Carol's cool fingers wrapped around Bill's hand. "Do you think it's the same guy?"

Bill's brows scrunched together, "These many months? It can't be related."

Carol answered, "Well, you should mention it to Cindy. She's refusing the leave the hospital until she talks to you. Oh, and there's a cop outside your door."

Bill's eyes widened, "Am I under arrest?"

"No, protection. That's all I can find out."

Bill yawned and grabbed the remote next to his bed. The television's light flickered around the dimly lit room. He turned on the local news. A picture of the Clark and Company entrance was framed in a photo behind the newscaster.

The newscaster said, "We don't know who the hero is behind these doors. One source claimed the manager single-handedly killed four assailants with their own weapons, and his bare hands. Clark and Company has not made a statement to the press. We do know the name of the deceased employee. Lori Davis. She had been with the company for five years and was pregnant with her first child."

Carol gasped, and Bill turned off the television and turned his back to Carol, ignoring the pain in his side. He felt her arm wrap around his shoulder, and her tears fall on his neck. Streams of salty tears flowed from his eyes.

Bill whispered, "I need to be alone."

Carol kissed the side of his head and said, "I'm so sorry. I know you didn't want her family finding out this way."

Bill begged, "Please."

Carol removed her arm, and Bill listened to her high heels click along the floor, and then the room door opened and shut. Bill closed his eyes and allowed the exhaustion from the pain medicine to take over. He was just drifting off to sleep when he heard the door open. Carol was arguing with another woman.

"You can't go in here. He needs his rest."

The stranger responded, "I'm aware. I'll be in and out before you know it. Please, the longer I wait, the less he'll remember. Especially on those pain pills."

Carol argued, "It isn't a good time."

The stranger insisted, "There'll never be a good time. I'm sorry, but this is for his safety. Until we identify who these men are with, he's in great danger."

There was silence, and then the door closed. Bill heard somebody sit down in the chair next to him. He pretended to be asleep. A hand grasped his shoulder and shook him. Bill quickly rolled over, glared at the stranger, and winced.

The woman had her black hair pulled back into a ponytail. She wore a khaki dress suit that accentuated her curves. She sat with her muscular legs crossed and a tablet of paper on her knee. She appeared unfazed by Bill's look.

"Good, you're awake. My name is Cindy Isabel Abrams."

The woman's pleasant demeanor had no effect on Bill's mood. "Perhaps you didn't hear my friend in the doorway. I'm not in the mood to talk."

The woman dropped her pad of paper in the satchel that hung from her shoulder. She bent forward and gently squeezed Bill's forearm.

"I am sorry for your loss. It's my job to find the killer of your fiancée and child."

Bill answered, "I thought I already took care of that."

Cindy sat back up. "Yes, you appear to have been quite thorough with the assailants."

Bill grunted.

"Can you tell me what the men told you?"

Bill stared up at the ceiling. "They wanted to know about my brother. When I told him I didn't have a brother, the man claimed Harold Brown from Parabolic Defense Systems was my brother. I smarted off and told him to call Forbes, and he shot Lori."

Bill began to cry.

Cindy's voice was compassionate, "Mr. Johnson, please don't blame yourself. These men have ties to a terrorist group. I doubt your joke killed your fiancée. They use death as a means of control. He would have shot her even if you had told him a location, just to be sure you were telling the truth."

Bill took a couple of jagged breaths and asked, "But, why me? I don't have a brother."

Cindy answered, "We have some theories, but I'm not at liberty to say. It could be a case of mistaken identity."

Bill grumbled, "What do you mean could be? What else could it be?"

"We're working on it. You work in an investment house. Perhaps their plan was to gain access to your systems, and the brother angle was their means of breaking you down. Obviously, they didn't expect your response."

"Do you know the man's name that killed Lori?"

Cindy nodded, "I do, but I'm not allowed to share that information."

"Why not?"

Cindy tapped the side of her chair, "It's need to know. Frankly, Mr. Johnson, the less you know about this situation, the better. We don't know if the people behind these men will try again, but the more we keep you out of the loop, the more likely they'll count their losses and move on."

Bill raised his bed up and stared into Cindy's eyes. "If there is someone behind this. I want him or her. I want to make them pay. They took everything from me."

Cindy stood and took Bill's hand. "I know how you feel, I really do. Please, let me handle this. I know how to deal with these people. I promise you'll have your justice."

Bill's voice was cold, "I'd rather have revenge."

Cindy let go of his hand. "Take my advice, Mr. Johnson. Get some professional help and learn how to forgive and let this go. These men have no conscience. They don't care about your pain or your anger. You'll only hurt yourself holding on to it. I promise they won't get away with what they've done."

Bill sat all the way up and ignored the pain pushing past his drugs. "I'm holding you responsible. I better hear something, or I'll come looking for you."

Cindy placed both hands on his guardrail and leaned close to his face. "Don't forget who you're talking to. I'm one of the good guys, but you don't want me for an enemy. I said I would take care of this, and I will."

She stood back up. "Normally, I don't follow-up with civilians involved in these matters, but I can see you'll need to know when it's over. I promise you'll be hearing back from me."

Bill's lips curved down, "Good."

Cindy walked over to the door and turned. "Mr. Johnson, take some time off, heal up both physically and mentally. You've been through a lot. I promise you can trust me."

Bill nodded, and Cindy left the room.

Bill laid back in his bed and closed his eyes. Soon the odor of antiseptic was replaced with a cool breeze and the smell of pine and oak.

CHAPTER 5

Bill blinked, shook his head, and looked around again. The low gray clouds and cold air told him to expect snow. Frost crusted the brown leaves on the forest floor along an almost imperceptible walking trail. Gray, leafless trees surrounded him for as far as he could see.

Bill mumbled, "I must be losing my mind. I can't be here and in the hospital."

He felt the soft wolf's fur hanging from his shoulders and the sharp axes nestled in their straps on his waist. Bill ran his finger down the front of a blade, and blood trickled to the ground.

"It feels so real, but they can't both be true."

A wisp of smoke far ahead caught his eye, and he began walking towards it. The crunch of the forest floor echoed around him. He slowed his pace and stopped well short of a clearing.

A large man with long, wavy red hair and a thick red beard sat by the fire. He was bare-chested and wore a bearskin off his shoulders, much like Bill's wolfskin. A large, two-handed battle ax leaned against the log he was sitting on. The man looked up from the fire and began to sniff the air.

"Brother, come sit by the fire. It's much warmer than from behind the trees."

Bill hesitated.

The large stranger hollered, "I can smell you from here. Don't you recognize your own brother?"

Bill hesitantly stepped out from behind the tree.

The man motioned Bill over, "There you are, come, sit."

Bill walked over and sat on a rock next to the large man.

"I am William of Oden."

The stranger laughed, "Of course you are. You really don't recognize me?"

Bill slowly shook his head.

"I'm Harold, your brother. It has been a long time, but I thought you would remember me."

Bill looked down at the fire while he spoke, "I didn't know I had a brother. To be honest, I'm not sure of anything at the moment. One minute I'm in the hospital, the next minute I'm here. I don't understand."

Harold spoke softly, "Yes, Joshua, that old wizard."

"Who?"

Harold reached over, grabbed Bill's knee and gave it a shake as he spoke, "Joshua, he's a powerful wizard who can play tricks with the mind."

Harold released Bill's knee, and Bill leaned in toward Harold. "What sort of tricks?"

Harold leaned closer to Bill and whispered, "Like making two brothers forget about each other."

Bill sat back upright. "That's ridiculous. Why would this man, if he exists, care if we're together?"

Harold looked around the woods and then answered, "Because we're not only brothers. We're Berserkers. One Berserker can take on a small regiment, but two Berserkers have taken out small armies. No king could defeat us if we were to fight together."

Bill sat quietly for a moment and warmed his hands near the fire. He finally answered, "I, for one, don't want to be a king or a conqueror. The love of my life and my child were killed by raiders or terrorists. My world is upside down, and I don't know what is real anymore. I only know she's gone, and somebody is responsible."

"I can help you. That's what brothers do."

Bill pulled his hands back and looked into Harold's blue eyes. "Thanks, all the same. I'll have my revenge. Besides, you said yourself, I can take out a regiment, what is one man to me?"

Harold asked, "What if you run into Joshua?"

Bill pulled out his axes, and Harold's hand extended towards his weapon but did not grasp it.

Bill answered, "Then I will kill the man who kept me from my brother. I'm tired of people separating me from my family."

Harold's hand returned to his side, and Bill returned his weapons to their proper resting place.

Harold spoke, "Then, I wish you Godspeed. Keep following the path, and you will find your answers. Where will I find you when you've finished your quest?"

"I am a child of Helvsgud. I'll return to the village once this is done."

"Very well. I'll wait there."

Bill stood, "Let the king know you're my brother. He will treat you well."

"Many thanks, brother."

Harold stood and locked Bill in a bear hug. Once he was free, Bill began back down the frozen path. Light snow had started to fall, but Bill could still find his way forward. The entire forest looked grayer, more dead as the white snow formed a thin, white blanket on the ground. Before much longer, the trees began to look more like shadows as night approached.

Up ahead, Bill could make out a large fire, and he quickened his pace. He boldly walked upon an older man. He wore a flax coat with a hood. His hair was gray, and his face held a few wrinkles that peeked out from the shadows of his hidden face.

Bill asked, "May I join you?"

The stranger answered, "Of course. What is your name?"

"I am William son of Oden, protector of Helvsgud."

Bill could see a smile in the shadows of his cloak.

"My name amuses you?"

The stranger answered, "My, how you've grown."

Bill stared intently at the stranger, "Do I know you?"

The stranger continued, "When I knew you, everyone called you Billy, and then Bill."

Bill sat down next to the stranger without being invited and stared hard into his eyes. Something seemed familiar about them. He remembered seeing them across from him in an office in the orphanage, but then again in the Viking village.

Bill said, "Perhaps you can help me. I have memories, many memories. Of this place, and another. A place with offices, hospitals, and cars."

The man nodded his head. "Yes, I know of that place. Both exist. One in your mind, and the other here on earth. You must have been through a great trauma to be in both places."

"Yes," answered Bill.

"Here and there?" asked the man.

Bill answered. "Yes. I don't know which is real, but I feel like I'm living two nightmares."

The man answered, "I can help you, but you must find me in that other place. There I am called Joshua Zeev."

Bill leaped to his feet and drew his axes. Joshua quickly stood and pulled his sword.

Bill growled, "Liar. Harold warned me about you. How can you be from these lands with a name like Joshua Zeev?"

Joshua answered calmly. "Look who's so smart, Bill. What else did Harold tell you?"

"All that I need to know. You're a wizard, a trickster, and you kept us apart and wiped my memory of him."

Joshua lowered his sword but kept it in his hand. "Your brother is partly correct. I did keep you apart, but not because I'm a wizard. I'm a doctor. We used to be close, you and I. We were like a family. Your brother was in another place, another land if you will. I traveled to help him like I had helped you, but things did not go as planned. I could not return. So, I had your memories of me hidden away. Now, it appears something has unleashed them."

Bill swung his axes twice. "Why should I believe you."

Joshua shrugged, "Why would I lie?"

Bill hollered, "Because you're a liar."

Bill's axes swung towards Joshua, and he deflected both with his sword. Bill's world turned crimson, and he growled, "You will pay with your life."

Joshua pleaded, "Listen to me, you must find me when you wake up. If you don't, you could be in great danger."

Bill stopped. "From whom?"

"Yourself."

Bill howled and dove towards Joshua. A bright light flashed between them. Bill's body jumped, and he blinked. A dim light remained, and he blinked again. The familiar smell of antiseptic told Bill he was back in his hospital room. His eyes darted around as he attempted to get his bearings.

A new nurse walked in, "Oh good, you're awake. Your surgeon is here. Hang tight."

The nurse left the room and a few moments later returned. A man in a white lab coat followed her into the room. He was at least as tall as Bill, but lanky and wore gold rim glasses. Judging from his graying hairline, Bill assumed the doctor was in his late fifties or early sixties. The doctor walked up to him, gently pulled down the sheets, and started removing the bandages before saying a word.

Finally, he spoke, "I'm Lewis Sundberg. You're quite a lucky man. No organ damage, some minor muscle damage. I would release you tonight, but I hear you don't have family in the area."

Bill answered, "Yea, I have a few friends."

Dr. Sundberg spoke without looking up. "Are you close to the young African American woman I saw in here most of the day?"

Bill said, "She's my administrator and a friend."

The doctor looked over at the nurse. "Betty, remind me to fire my administrator. She's obviously falling down on the job."

Betty let out a short laugh.

Bill answered, "I'm serious."

Dr. Sundberg turned to Bill with a smile on his face. "About her being just an administrator?"

"Yes." Answered Bill, annoyed.

"And you're friends?"

"Yes, only friends. My fiancée was killed in the office attack."

Dr. Sundberg scowled and looked away. "I'm sorry, I didn't make the connection."

Bill remained quiet as the doctor finished his work.

Dr. Sundberg said, "I think we can release you tomorrow. I've put in a prescription for some NSAIDs and opioids. I would use the NSAIDs and only use the opioids at night, and then only if you really need one."

"I can do that."

Dr. Sundberg continued, "I would feel better if somebody would stay with you for the first few days. The injury is not bad, but you don't strike me as the kind of guy that sits still. If you tear some of the stitches, I want to know you have somebody that can get you in here."

"I can arrange it." Said Bill.

Dr. Sundberg nodded and headed towards the door. He stopped and turned, "Sorry for your loss."

The doctor left the room.

Betty walked over, "Do you need anything to help you sleep?"

"I don't think I want to sleep with the dreams I've been having."

Betty padded his arm. "You've been through a lot. I'll give you something that should help you rest without the nightmares."

Bill looked up at the ceiling, "That would be a welcome change."

Betty walked over to the computer stand and began typing into the keyboard. Her voice rose above the clicks, "What will you do when you get out?"

Bill answered. "I have some people I need to find. We have some unfinished business."

"Well, don't work too hard. I'll be back with your medicine."

Chapter 6

Bill sat in his recliner, drumming his fingers. A golf tournament announcer droned from the tv. He heard Carol starting the clothes washer.

Bill hollered, "Carol, please, you don't have to do that."

"I know, I want to. Besides, the doctor told you to take it easy. You can't be bending over lifting anything for at least a week."

Bill sighed and looked up at the cathedral ceiling. His eyes trailed along the far wall of the living room. He scowled at the thin layer of dust rested on his bookcase, television, and even picture frames. Carol walked around the corner of the kitchen. "What's wrong?"

"I didn't realize how filthy I'd let my place get."

Carol looked around the room. "What?"

"Dust, there's dust everywhere, and the pillows are all disorganized."

Carol walked back into the kitchen and hollered at Bill from the other side of the wall, "I can see you're going to be a handful."

Bill answered, "You don't have to stay here. I can take care of myself."

Carol walked back in with a glass of sweet tea and one of Bill's pain pills. She answered, "That's what worries me, and your doctor. You'll be in the emergency room in a day if I leave you to yourself."

Bill took his pill and followed it up with his tea chaser. He put down the glass, "Then you really won't like what I'm about to tell you."

Carol sat down on the couch next to him and leaned in, "What are you planning?"

"I'm just going for a little drive tomorrow."

Carol responded, "Don't make me hide your keys."

Bill got silent, picked up the television remote, and turned on the golf channel. He spoke to the golf pro taking a chip shot. "You can't stop me. The doctor cleared me to drive."

Carol protested, "You're not going into work."

Bill's forehead wrinkled, "No, what? Why would I?

Carol's finger pressed against his chest. "Where do you think you're going?"

Bill turned his attention to Carol and looked into her concerned eyes. "I need to talk to Dr. Adam about this Joshua guy."

"You know that could all be trauma-induced."

"I know. I just, well, I need to know. Do I have a brother out there somewhere, and if there was a man named Joshua, what did he do?"

Carol removed her finger, "I can come along."

"No, this is something I need to do on my own. Don't worry, I'll take it easy."

Carol's right foot began to tap. "The orphanage is an hour and a half from here."

Bill looked back at the television, "I'll stop and take breaks."

Carol lightly tapped his temple, "You know, for a smart man, you sure can play the fool sometimes. If the painkillers don't make you wreck, the pain will."

"Well, that's why you're here, to keep me straight."

Carol got up and headed into the guest room, mumbling so Bill could hear. "Darn fool, he's going to get himself killed."

Bill hollered, "I'm not that stupid."

Carol marched back in and plopped down on the couch. "Listen to me, Mr. Columbia Graduate. If you aren't careful, you'll tear those stitches and ram that car of yours into someone or something at seventy miles per hour."

Bill took a sip of tea and put it down. "Well, Joshua said if I didn't find him soon, I could be in real danger. Besides, if Harold Brown is my brother, these guys could come back for me. I need to try and figure out what's going on."

"Why not just go away for a little while and rest?"

Bill sat quietly for a moment and focused his attention on the golfer teeing off. Then he said, "I might do that. John has wanted me to take a trip with him to the mountain house he and Rhonda had built."

"Oh, really?" replied Carol, "I didn't know you two had become buddies."

"Well, when you set up a tax-free offshore retirement fund, some people appreciate the effort. I'm not sure it's all about the money, though. He's been bugging me to get back into church ever since I've met him."

Carol answered, "That doesn't sound like bad advice."

Bill rolled his eyes, "Whatever. Anyway, maybe we can go up there."

"When you say we, I hope you're not including me on your vacation."

Bill's eyes widened. "What? I thought you'd want to come."

Carol reached over and grabbed Bill's hand. "I do. I want to be here to help you through this, but I need to get back to the office before too long. Besides, you'll have John, and who'll tell you what's happening at the office if I'm not there?"

Bill took his hand back, "Okay. I'll call John in a minute. First, I need to call the director of the orphanage. Adam and I go back to my childhood. If anyone knows about this Joshua, it's him."

"Don't get up."

"Thanks." Responded Bill.

Carol brought Bill the phone and headed in the direction of her room. Bill muted the television and dialed the number to the North Carolina Children's Home and asked to speak to Dr. Adam Murray. Bill began to feel a little drowsy when an old but familiar voice grabbed his attention.

"Billy, how are you?"

Bill cleared his throat, "It's Bill, now. I'm good, Dr. Murray. How are you?"

"Please, call me Adam. It's been a long time."

Bill replied, "It has been. I was thinking of dropping by tomorrow, would that be alright?"

"How long will you be in the area?"

Bill answered, "Oh, it's just a short hello. I've had some strange dreams as of late, and I'd like to talk to you about them."

Adams's voice seemed to tense up, "Dreams, what sort of dreams."

Bill paused.

Adam asked, "Are you still there?"

"Yes. Just memories, I think, of the orphanage. I wanted to check some things out."

Adam asked, "Are you close by? A visit seems like a lot of trouble for some dreams. Perhaps you could tell me about them now."

Bill responded slowly, "I'm in the area for a short time. I thought it was a good excuse to say hello."

Adam's perked up. "Wonderful. I hope I can talk you into staying longer. Do you know when you'll be here?"

"No. Sometime in the afternoon. I hope that's alright."

Adam replied, "Certainly, my boy. I look forward to seeing you."

Bill hung up, quietly lowered his recliner, and grunted as he rose from the chair. He snuck into his master bathroom, and eased the door close. After washing his hands, he started to exit when he spied Carol. She blocked his only egress from the bedroom.

"Uh oh, I'm busted," joked Bill.

"Should you be standing by yourself?"

"Carol, you need to relax. If I need help, I'll holler, yell or scream. Lori doesn't baby me this much."

At the sound of his own words, darkness crossed over Bill's face. He looked down at the floor, pushed his way past Carol, and sat back down in his chair.

Carol walked up, squeezed his arm, and whispered, "I'm sorry."

Bill looked up at her, "I'm the one who should be sorry. You didn't do anything wrong. I appreciate your concern. I just hadn't thought about the whole affair while we were talking. My comment brought everything back."

"Are you doing alright?"

"I'll be okay. I just can't believe I forgot about Lori for a moment. I guess I was too focused on my phone call."

"With John?" asked Carol.

"No, Adam at the orphanage."

Carol moved back to the couch and leaned towards Bill, "What did he say."

Bill's brow furrowed, "Nothing exactly. It was more the way he said things. I mentioned I wanted to visit, that I had had some weird dreams. After that, it felt like he was trying to nail down where I was. He wanted to know if I was nearby, how long I would be staying, the exact time of my arrival tomorrow."

Carol sat back, "That just sounds like an old friend who's hoping to spend some time with you."

"Maybe. I guess my talk with Cindy at the hospital has me looking over my shoulder. Dr. Adam would never do anything to hurt me. After all, he was the one who got me into the Columbia Business School. I'm his poster child for other children."

Carol stood up, "Well, I'm going to grab a nap if I'm not needed right now. Why don't you call John? I think you could use a vacation."

"Good idea."

Carol left, and Bill dialed the number.

"How's my favorite superhero?"

Bill replied, annoyed, "I'm no hero, much less super."

"Carol told me some of what happened. I'm just trying to cheer you up."

"Do me a favor, don't try so hard."

John's voice got softer, "I know you feel like you failed Lori and your baby, but do me a favor, think about what I'm going to tell you.

"I know it doesn't seem like much, but if you hadn't done what you did, everyone could be dead. You, Carol, everybody. I hate that Lori was killed, but I'm thankful you survived, and the other worker's families are grateful for your actions."

Bill acquiesced, "Thanks. Hey, any chance the two of us can go to the mountain house? Things are getting weirder, and I need to get out of here."

"Weirder than the shooting?"

"Yea. I'd rather talk up there instead of on the phone."

John said, "We can leave tonight if you're up for it."

"Well, that's tempting, but I'm driving up to Thomasville tomorrow."

"Wow, I didn't think you'd heal up that fast."

"Oh, I didn't say I wasn't hurting. I need to visit the orphanage. I have questions about why I went crazy and killed those men, and I think the orphanage may hold some answers."

John said, "The press said the police have closed the investigation and are considering this a robbery gone bad."

Bill was quiet for just a moment. "Well, if that's what the press is reporting, go with what they are telling you. I haven't heard anything from law enforcement."

John replied, "That seems strange."

"Yea, well, I've been sort of doped up the past twenty-four hours. Speaking of, my pain medicine is kicking in, and I'm feeling pretty tired. I need to get some rest before tomorrow's little drive. I'll see you in a couple of days."

John answered, "Alright, see you then, Bud."

Bill hung up the phone. He quietly got out of his chair and held his side as he slowly made his way back to his bedroom, closed the door, and turned on the light. Bill noticed the pregnancy test on Lori's side of the bed. He turned the light off, climbed into his bed, buried his face in his satin pillow, and cried himself to sleep.

CHAPTER 7

Bill gently massaged his side near the bullet wound. He jerked and gasped for a moment. An aged, dark mahogany desk sat empty in front of him. Although he was a grown man, he still felt like a little boy, called to the administrator's office for something he had done.

He recalled putting a dead mouse in the office of the cook and smiled. The poor woman hated mice, and the scene she caused after sitting on one was the talk of the orphanage for weeks. It had been worth the month-long kitchen duty after Bill was found to be the source of her consternation.

The old wooden floors and oak paneling in Adam's office looked darker. Despite its clean appearance, the room smelled musty, mustier than Bill remembered. He stood up and walked over to the large double-pane windows and looked out at some of the children playing in the cold fall air. The long shadows from the trees seemed to envelop the light. The children ignored the darkness and squealed with delight as they enjoyed a game of duck, duck goose.

A door opened, and Bill turned to find Dr. Adam Murray. His black hair was now mostly gray and thinner.

He was shorter than Bill remembered. The two men approached one another, embraced, and Bill quickly gasped.

They released, and Adam smacked Bill on the shoulders. "Look at you. What a fine man you've become."

Bill regained his breath, "You haven't aged so bad yourself."

Adam started towards his desk and pointed Bill to the chair he previously sat in, "Oh, don't let the innocence going on outside fool you. It gets harder and harder to keep up with this lot. I tell you, Bill, I don't know if the kids are more rambunctious or if I'm getting older."

"Maybe a little of both."

Adam chuckled, "Indeed. So, tell me, what have you been up to?"

"I was on Wall Street for a while."

Adam nodded, "Yes. Tell me, why did you leave? I thought that was the dream for every investor."

Bill shrugged, "Yea, well, it isn't as romantic as the movies make it out to be. Don't get me wrong, I had a good time, but the pressures get to everybody. You know the old saying, big risk, and big reward. Sadly, one can only handle the stress of big risks for so long."

"You showed a lot of wisdom on knowing when to leave."

Bill looked up at the old copper stamped ceiling, "Perhaps. I took a job down here at Clark and Company."

Adam said nothing.

Bill looked at Adam, "What?"

Adam asked quietly, "That was you? You're the man who saved those office workers?"

Tears formed and Bill's vision blurred.

Adam continued, "The news reported the man had lost his fiancée and unborn child in the attack. I'm so sorry."

Tears began to flow from Bill's eyes before he could stop himself. He took a deep breath and then spoke. "I wanted to save her, but I couldn't."

"But you saved so many. If you hadn't been there, they might all be dead."

Bill stood up and began to pace behind the chair.

He wiped the tears from his cheeks and said, "That's why I'm here. So many things happened that day. I changed, and I don't know what I've become."

"Anyone would change after such an event. I hope you're getting counseling."

Bill stopped, put his hands on the back of the chair, and leaned towards Adam, "That's not what I mean. I changed during the attack. I became enraged. Physically, psychologically. My vision turned crimson. It was almost like I could see the blood running through my eyes. I could hear my heartbeat so loud that I barely heard the man threatening me."

Bill lifted his shirt to show Adam his bandage. "The bullet that did this. I liked the pain; it was almost euphoric. I wanted them to shoot me again. And then I attacked the man that killed Lori, my fiancée. I beat his head in until there was nothing left. It wasn't just pure anger; it was fun like the kids enjoy playing outside."

Bill lowered his shirt, and Adam leaned forward and pointed to the chair, "Please, sit down. I have a few things to tell you."

Bill interrupted Adam as he sat down. "I'm not done."

"Go ahead."

"Afterwards. I started having weird dreams. At first, I just thought it was about losing Lori because she was killed in my dreams. But then, I met people I remember nothing about. A brother, and a man named Joshua. Joshua told me if I didn't find him immediately, I was in great danger."

Adam asked, "Did Joshua say why?"

Bill paused. Small beads of sweat began to form on Adam's forehead. Bill pressed, "What do you know? Who was Joshua, and do I have a brother?"

Adam walked to the front of his desk, and sat on the corner. He crossed his arms like he used to do when he had bad news to give Bill. Bill sat back down.

"You do have a brother."

"So the killer was right."

"Excuse me? What did the man tell you?"

Bill answered, "He said he was looking for Harold Brown. I told him I didn't have a brother."

Adam dropped his arms to his side, "What did this man look like?"

"Why?"

Adam hurried back around his desk and grabbed a pad of paper and a pen from a drawer. "Please, I'll explain in a moment."

Bill answered, "It's like I told Cindy from the FBI, they all wore masks. He had a British accent. That's all I can really say."

Adam nodded and continued, "Were any of the men smoking a cigar?"

"What? No."

"Are you sure?"

Bill's voice went up an octave, "I would remember a guy in a ski mask smoking a cigar. What's going on?"

Adam put down his writing implements. "Your brother and Joshua are in danger."

Bill asked, "Is that why I don't remember them?"

Adam took a long breath and let it out. His shoulders lowered. "In a manner of speaking. Harold Brown is your half-brother. You both share the same mother. She allowed Harold to be put up for adoption."

"Why?"

Adam answered, "I'm afraid I'm not at liberty to say. Please trust me when I tell you that your brother and his parents tried to adopt you. It got to the point that Joshua and I had to intervene for fear your birth mother's family would take you from us. You were safer here than with that clan."

"You mean you kept me from my forever family, my real family?"

Adam shook his head, "No. In a manner of speaking, I mean, but not every family is a family you want to be a part of. They were trouble. There were cases of incest, rape, and beatings within the extended family, and we wanted to protect you from that. Your mother demanded we protect you."

"Why couldn't she take care of me?"

Adam spoke softly, "Your mother was a special lady, but she had been abused. Her mind was not right, and she knew she couldn't take care of you."

Bill looked down at the floor and started to count the number of knots in the wood.

Adam continued, "Joshua was your psychiatrist."

Bill looked up and asked, "Why don't I remember him?"

"Please, have patience. I'll tell you everything I know.

"You were a furious young man. Well, I should say you could be. Some of the staff thought you were possessed. When you got angry, your voice would deepen, and your body would exhibit almost superhuman strength. Everything came to a head the day an older bully named Bobby was beating you up outside. You became incensed and broke his arm.

"We knew we had to try something drastic before you ended up in jail. Joshua built a world in your mind through hypnotherapy. It was a Viking world because you were always fascinated with their stories. Your mother and her family are from Denmark, so we thought that would make a strong connection in your mind. Joshua called your angry side the Berserker, like the warriors of old. Over time he helped you see you didn't need to fight a Berserker war, and the two of you locked the beast away in your mind."

Bill's forehead creased, and his voice rose, "Then why don't I remember any of this?"

Adam answered, "Joshua was called away to help with Harold. Your brother was worse than you, and his parents begged him to come and help. Joshua thought he would do for Harold what he did for you and would be back in a year. Unfortunately, a year turned to two years, then three, and then we both knew he would not be coming back.

"Rather than try and explain how Joshua had left you for your half-brother, Joshua talked me into compartmentalizing that memory into your subconscious. He was concerned that losing both him and your brother might cause you to relapse to your violent side."

Bill's fingers drummed against the chair's armrest. "So, I was close to Joshua?"

"He was like a father to you."

Bill's breathing began to become shallower, quicker. His voice deepened slightly, "You mean, you both hid away all my good memories because you thought no memories were better?"

Adam's voice was hesitant, "We thought we were doing what was best."

Bill's voice rose in volume, "Best?"

Bill grabbed the armrests and tore them from the seat. He dropped them and then buried his head in his hands and wept. In a few seconds, he could feel Adam rubbing his back.

Adam spoke softly, "I'm so sorry, we didn't know this would happen."

Bill's muffled voice asked, "What am I?"

Adam replied confidently, "You're still the same man."

"Am I? I just tore apart your chair."

"Chairs can be replaced."

Bill's voice was urgent, "But what if I didn't stop at the furniture? What about Joshua's warning?"

Adam returned to his desk and began writing, "I'll contact Joshua and see what he tells me."

"So, you know where he is?"

"I know how to contact him."

"Then you know where he is?"

Adam looked Bill in the eye, "No."

"I don't understand. Why wouldn't you know?"

"Bill, the man after Joshua, and Harold is extremely dangerous. If I knew where they were, that could put the orphanage and me in danger."

Bill's voice softened, "That's why they came after me. They assumed Harold or Joshua had contacted me."

Adam nodded, "They probably thought they would try and bring you to their location for safety."

"Then why didn't they believe me when I told them I didn't know?"

Adam's head drooped, "I wish I knew."

Bill asked, "So, what am I supposed to do now?"

"You're welcome to stay here at the orphanage if you like. It's safe enough, and maybe I can help you with these memories of yours. What you need most of all is time away from this tragedy so you can grieve and let your emotions work themselves out."

Bill thought for a moment, "Thanks for the offer. I already have a trip to the mountains planned with a friend of mine. It's quiet, and he has a good ear. I think that's probably the best plan. I may come back for a visit when I return."

Adam asked, "Where are you staying?"

Bill looked hard at Adam, "I don't want to say. Like you said, the more we know, the more dangerous things can be. At least I know some of the reasons why I'm in danger. If you need me, call my cell phone. Do you need the number?"

Adam said, "I saved the number after you called."

"Good. Well, I should go. I have a lot to think about, and if I'm honest, the pain in my side is starting to get worse."

Adam stood with Bill, and the two shook hands. Adam said, "Please come visit, don't be a stranger."

"Something tells me I'll be back."

Bill tapped on his steering wheel as the orphanage faded from view in his review mirror. He glanced up at the sky, "If you're there, why would you do this? My family, and now my childhood? How can you possibly be good and let these things happen?"

Bill cranked up his radio as he merged on to interstate eighty-five south. He frequently checked his mirror and memorized every car that passed.

Chapter 8

The doorbell rang, and Carol hollered, "I got it."

"Thanks," replied Bill.

He stood there taking inventory of his suitcase and overheard John and Carol talking in the great room. Bill walked into the master bathroom and confirmed all his items were in his shaving kit. He stopped, looked back at the bedroom, and his heart sank. It was just two weeks ago; Lori and he had been doing the very same thing for their weekend beach trip.

Muscles tightened, and pain pierced his side as tears trickled down his cheeks. He blinked and tightened his fist to control the pain. Carol clearing her throat caught his attention.

"Are you sure you are up for this?"

Bill grimaced, "Yea. Adam said I needed to get away and give my head time to sort things out."

"But there? There are memories in the mountains too."

"There are memories everywhere. At least I can relax and talk to John."

"You can talk to me."

Bill walked over and gave Carol a hug. "It's not the same."

Carol turned in Bill's direction as he zipped his suitcase shut, "I thought we were friends."

"We are. I don't know, it's different with John."

"Don't tell me it's because he's a guy."

Bill plopped the suitcase on the floor, "It's because he's married."

Carol said nothing, and Bill grunted as he left the bedroom with the suitcase in tow.

John asked, "Are we doing this?"

"You know we are."

"Can I help you with the suitcase?"

Bill hesitated and then handed John the handle.

Carol gave Bill a hug goodbye, and the men headed towards the mountain sanctuary. Neither person said much on the drive up.

John pulled up to the gated community in West Jefferson. He reached out to punch in his code but stopped, and then turned to Bill. "I have to ask. What's the deal with Carol?"

Bill's eyebrows rose, "What do you mean?"

"I'm simply curious about Carol. Why was she there this morning?"

"Not that it's any of your business, but the doctor wanted somebody around to make sure I didn't do too much. She volunteered."

"So, you guys are close?"

Bill started tapping the armrest on the door. "Look, she's my admin and my friend, ok? She's the closest thing I have to family now, besides you."

John put up his hands, "Ok. Sorry. I just wanted to make sure you weren't making any bad decisions in your grief."

"Give me a little credit."

"I'm sorry."

John reached back out the window, punched in the code, and the cedar gates slowly swung open. Bill looked out over the view as the SUV climbed the curvy road to the top of the hill. With each foot higher, he could feel his body relaxing. There was something about a mountain view that helped him breathe easier.

The house came into view. It's beautiful rock entryway and the valley's picturesque farms below put a smile on Bill's face. The pain that had radiated in his side faded a little. John pulled up and stopped in the gravel driveway.

John said, "Well, let's get unloaded and decide what to do with the day."

"That sounds like a plan." Responded Bill.

They entered the home. No matter how many times Bill had been there, the grand living room with tongue and groove walls and ceiling always took him back to his favorite ski lodges. He walked into his usual bedroom on the main floor. To Bill's surprise, he did not feel sad. It almost felt like old times before he and Lori started to date. Bill sat on the edge of the bed for a couple of minutes and looked around the room.

John hollered from the main room, "Do you want a beer, or do you want to grab lunch?"

Bill wanted a beer, but he had not eaten yet, and a beer would go right to his head. He walked out of the bedroom, "Let's do both."

A short while later, the two men were sitting in King George's Pub in downtown West Jefferson. John lifted his mug of a local brew, and Bill followed suit.

John said, "To good friends in times of grief. May we always be here for each other."

Bill nodded, and they clinked their mugs, and Bill took a big swallow. "That's just what I need."

Both men ordered their favorite burgers, and Bill sat back and watched the handful of patrons at the bar. Most appeared to be locals sharing gossip with the bartender.

John broke in, "So, are you planning on going back to your old job, or do you think you'll take a longer break than just a couple of weeks?"

Bill shrugged, "Who knows. I'm taking life one day at a time right now. Did I mention I went to the orphanage yesterday?"

John nodded his head.

Bill leaned closer to John and lowered his voice. "I've been having these crazy dreams; about people I don't know or shouldn't know. Adam told me they had been part of my childhood."

"Why didn't you remember them?"

Bill continued, "That's a long story. Anyway, they may be connected to Lori's murder. Adam said I could be in danger, as well."

John drew closer to Bill, "Are we in danger?"

"I don't think so. At least, Adam seemed relieved I was leaving Charlotte. I didn't say where I was going, so it isn't like anyone knows where we are beside Carol and Rhonda, and I think we can trust the two of them."

John looked around the bar a few times. "I wish you had told me before we left."

"Does that mean you want to go back home?"

John shook his head. "No, but I have people, security. Being head of operations and traveling into some hostile countries means I'm looked after. I could have insured our safety."

Bill picked up his mug, "Well, if you need to, call them up here. I think our anonymity is probably all we need from the way Adam reacted."

Bill took another long swallow, and John followed suit and then answered, "You seem very calm for a guy that was shot and then told the people involved may take another run at him."

Bill put down his beer. "Look, I have a lot on my mind. There's more happening that I don't want to talk about right now. Let's just say if anyone showed up, I'm not too worried about protecting us. What happened in the office was not a fluke, according to Adam. If I can find out who's behind this, I will make them pay for what happened to Lori."

"I thought you already did that."

"I think he was just the trigger man."

John's asked, "If you get that man, and then the one after that, and the next. How will it end?"

Bill's face darkened, "The same way it ended for his henchman, and the henchman after him, and on down the line."

Both men sat quietly, and their food soon arrived. They ate in silence and then drove back the short distance to the house.

As soon as they walked inside, John turned to Bill. "Are you really planning on killing this unknown Mr. Big, or whatever he calls himself?"

"I don't know. If he walked through that door right now, I would say yes. I just, I don't know. Can we drop it for now?"

John nodded his head. Both men walked over to the couches for their routine of sports watching and napping after a heavy lunch.

Bill's cellphone vibrated in his pocket. His leg jerked, and he opened his eyes. The scene of wooden walls and unfamiliar furniture temporarily disoriented him. He pulled his phone out of his pocket and mumbled into the receiver, "Yea."

Carol's voice whispered on the other end, "I need to talk to you."

Bill rubbed his eyes and blinked a couple of times. "Yea, go ahead."

Carol rushed her response, "You're getting fired."

Bill sat up, "What?"

Carol changed her tone, "Yes, Bob. I need those supplies sent here tomorrow. We have a new boss coming from London, and the Corporate heads want this place cleaned up and looking fresh."

Bill answered, "They can't do that."

John spoke up, "Do what?"

Bill ignored him.

Carol whispered, "I have a copy of your severance package. It's two years full salary and benefits, including bonuses based on last year's record commissions."

"So, they're paying me off. Why?"

Carol answered, "Give me a minute, I'll call you back."

The phone line went dead, and Bill stared blankly, holding his cell phone on his lap.

John spoke up, "What happened? You look like you've been gut-punched."

Bill blinked a couple of times and then looked over at John to answer. His cell phone rang, and he put his index finger up to John. Bill saw Carol's personal cell phone number and answered.

Bill asked, "Where are you?"

"Walking to my car for a coffee run."

"There's coffee in the building."

"Don't argue with me."

Bill complied, "Ok, what's going on?"

"The brass didn't like the publicity the attack brought."

Bill protested, "I didn't have any choice in the matter. What did they expect me to do, roll over and die?"

"I'm not sure. This is still a British company. They said they didn't like the fact that you killed four men with an assault rifle."

"That I took off one of the assailants."

Carol continued, "You're preaching to the choir. I say take the deal and leave this place. You don't need them hassling you about this anyway."

Bill looked over at John. John had his eyes stretched wide. Bill covered the receiver, "I got let go."

John mouthed, "Why?"

Bill held up his finger again.

Carol asked, "Are you still there."

"Yea, I'm just trying to understand what's happening. It seems very convenient that Lori is killed, and now they fire me."

Carol said, "Don't start down that damn fool conspiracy theory of yours. You told me last night Adam said some guy is looking for this Joshua and Harold, and now maybe you too."

"Maybe they're working together."

"Stop it. I know investors can be dirty, but where's the money trail? Nobody teams up with terrorists unless there is a lot of money involved. The only money I'm seeing is your parachute."

Bill responded, "Just because we can't see the money doesn't mean it isn't there."

Carol sounded exasperated, "Baby, this is your friend speaking to you. Take the money and run. You told me you had a nest egg already saved up. Well, take this, do your day trading and figure out what you want to do with the rest of your life."

Bill let out a sigh, "I wasn't planning on retiring in my thirties."

"Then don't. Just find something new."

"Thanks. I better go. John is about to explode with curiosity."

Carol replied, "Ok, call me later."

"I will."

They both hung up.

John immediately asked, "What is going on? You got fired?"

"Severance."

John asked, "What are you going to do?"

"I don't know."

CHAPTER 9

The flames licked at the darkness, and the light danced off Bill's eyes. Heat pressed against his face and the night air ran a cold breeze across his back. Bill placed his feet against the warm rock of the firepit. John's face stared through the flickering shadows and light. His eyes unwavering, waiting for an answer from Bill.

Bill stammered under the watchful eyes of his friend. "Look, I don't expect you to understand. You have Rhonda. You can't possibly know what it's like."

John's eyes softened, "You're right, I can't. Maybe I would be as angry as you, but this obsession with killing more people, it's not healthy."

Bill stared up at the stars. The remote mountain location seemed to open the heavens above the light of the fire. For a moment, Bill realized how small he was. He closed his eyes and saw Lori lying dead on the floor. His heartbeat began to grow louder. "They killed her."

"And you killed them."

Bill stood, shaking his head. The cold air blasted through his open coat, and he closed it and crossed his arms. He paced in short steps, not wandering far from the fire. "But I didn't get everybody. Somebody had to plan all of this. I wouldn't be practically hiding up here if that wasn't true."

John remained seated and replied, "True, but it's not your place to be the executioner."

Bill growled, "Why not? Why do I have to sit back and wait for justice from strangers?"

"Because we would fall into anarchy and war if everyone took matters into their own hands."

Bill waived John off. His frustration rose, and his heartbeat grew louder. He turned back to his friend and replied in a gravelly voice, "You don't know anything. I thought you, of all people, wouldn't be a coward. Standing by and letting others fight your battles."

Bill stormed away from the fire and paced around the yard in the darkness.

John stood up, "Bill, you're getting too worked up, you need to calm down."

Bill's muscles tingled, the pain in his side faded, and his anger grew. "Stop telling me what to do."

Bill bent over and ripped away a railroad tie from the flower bed. He flung it far down the hill until it landed with a thud and crunch at the edge of the dark woods. His body began to shake, his knees buckled, and pain flashed from his side. Bill collapse to the cold, wet ground.

John rushed over and knelt by him, "Are you alright?"

Bill began to weep. He felt John's arms hold him the way Adam used to when he was upset. The scene changed for a moment and Joshua held him on the playing field of the orphanage. Bill wiggled loose of John's embrace and looked at his friend wide-eyed. He gasped, "What's wrong with me?"

John answered in a soft voice. "I don't know. Let me help you back to the fire."

Bill shook his head and forced himself off the ground. His body felt heavy, and his muscles burned. He slid his cold hand under his shirt. To his relief he was not bleeding. Bill plodded over and collapsed in his chair. The warmth of the fire against his feet and legs began to loosen some of the stiffness. The two men sat in silence, staring at the blaze.

John finally asked, "Do you think you should go see Adam again?"

"I don't know. He said he was going to call me after he hears from Joshua. I guess he's having a tougher time finding him than I thought he would. Besides, the last thing I need to do is lose it in front of a bunch of kids."

"Yea. Hey, do you want to talk with my pastor?" offered John.

Bill scowled, "I gave that up years ago. Tell me, John, where is God, if he's around? Where was God when Lori was shot? Where was he when Joshua screwed with my head? Why would God even make me like this if I'm actually created?"

John sat silent.

Bill answered, "That's what I thought."

"Just because I don't know the answer doesn't mean there isn't one."

Bill replied, "I'll tell you what. If God will bring me somebody with some answers, and if he shows me why he did this to me, I'll come back to him."

John's eyes drilled into Bill's, "Who made you God?

"What?"

The flames reflected off John's eyes. "Why would the God of the universe bow to your demands?"

"I don't know. Look, I know the Bible says we will find God if we seek him with our whole heart. So, I'm open to what you and everyone else in my life have claimed again and again."

"And if that doesn't happen?"

Bill stood up. "I'm going to grab a beer. Do you want one?"

John nodded.

In a few minutes, Bill returned with two opened bottles. After he gave John his beer, he sat back down and took a long swallow.

He finally answered John, "If God leaves me blowing in the breeze, then I'll see what this Joshua character tells me. Maybe I'll do what he suggests. If not, I don't know, maybe find me a cabin with an internet connection and live alone off my investments."

"You'd be a hermit?"

"If I can't control myself, it would probably be safer for everyone to be isolated."

John raised his bottle, "From your lips to God's ear. For the record, I don't believe you should hide under a rock."

"We'll see."

The two quietly sipped their beers. Bill placed a couple of small limbs in the fire and put his feet as close as he dared to the flames. He pulled them back as the soles of his shoes began to smoke.

John stared at the sky and finally looked back at Bill and asked, "Will you keep the house?"

"I don't know. I can't think that far ahead. Maybe I'll sell it and buy one of the lots up here and be your neighbor."

"There are worse places to live."

"So, what's going on at your job?" asked Bill.

The two men talked about John's job, family, and Rhonda's plans for the mountain house until the fire died out. Bill was thankful for an hour or so of normalcy. Ready to fall asleep, he walked up the two flights of stairs to the main floor, exhausted.

Bill walked into his bedroom, took off his shoes, laid face-first into his pillow for a moment, and then started to snore. He soon found himself walking on the grounds of the orphanage as a child. Joshua was walking with him, holding his hand. Bill let go and skipped ahead.

"Are we going to the Viking village?" asked Bill.

"Would you like that?"

Bill responded, "Yes," and he twirled and danced beneath the blossoming trees.

Bill tripped, his body jerked, and he woke up on his bed in the mountain house. He slipped off his pants and slid under the blankets. "Who are you, Joshua?"

Chapter 10

Bill sipped his coffee at the oak dining table and looked past his friend through the picture window at the fall mountain morning. The low clouds partially covering the hills meant a temperature change was coming. Gray bare trees extended below the cloud line and into the brown valley below.

John sat holding Bill's phone, lost in thought as he read the document on its screen.

He put down the phone, "That seems more than generous."

Bill nodded in silence and stared blankly out the window.

"I thought you'd be relieved to finally hear from Clark and Company."

Bill looked over at John. "Sorry, I've got a lot on my mind."

"I understand," John took a sip of his coffee.

Bill asked, "Do you think I'll ever be alright?"

John reached over and grabbed his friend's forearm, "Look at me."

Bill looked into John's penetrating eyes.

"You're going to be fine. Will things be like they used to be? No, but everything changes, including us. Give yourself some time. Give God a chance."

John let go of Bill's arm, and Bill pulled it back.

Bill's fingers started to drum on the table. "Look, I know what I said last night, but so far, God hasn't shown up in my life since I was a kid. I've always taken care of myself, but now things are different. I'm told people screwed with my head. I'm not even sure who I am anymore."

John answered, "If you obsess over it, you may have bigger problems with your brain from all the added stress."

Bill took his phone back and slipped it into his pocket. "What do you suggest. Just sit around here and wait for a couple of men to show up wearing sunglasses on a mission from God?"

The doorbell rang. Bill and John's mouths dropped open.

John asked, "Aren't you going to answer that?"

"What for? This is your house."

John stood, "I'm not expecting anyone, are you?"

The doorbell rang again.

Bill pointed at the door, "Now who's overthinking. Just look out and see who it is."

John walked over and looked through the peephole, blinked, and looked again. The doorbell rang a third time, and John opened the door. Bill could hear a quiet exchange of greetings.

John looked over his shoulder, "They're here to see you."

Bill hesitated, but then stood and slowly walked towards the front door. When he was halfway across the room, John took a step back, and Bill froze in place. Two people stood on the front porch. The woman was close to Bill's age, but he thought she was possibly a little older. She was Bill's height, wore a khaki pantsuit, and was built like an athlete. Next to her stood a man that Bill guessed was in his late fifties. He was in decent shape for his age. He wore jeans, a flannel shirt, and a trucker's cap with a local bait shop's name. Both people wore sunglasses on this overcast morning.

John smiled and patted Bill on the back as they walked past each other. The two strangers held out identification.

The man said, "We're with the CIA. I'm agent Garcia Hernandez, and this is agent Darla Brown."

The woman removed her sunglasses and shook his hand. "I hope we haven't startled you. I imagine we're the last people you'd expect at your front door."

Bill asked, "How'd you get past the gate."

Garcia smiled and answered, "Please, Mr. Johnson. We're CIA."

"What do you want with me?"

Darla replied, "May we come in?"

"Sure."

The two agents came in and sat next to each other on the couch, and Bill took the loveseat.

John stepped over, "Do I need to leave?"

Darla answered, "Please, join us. This will impact you, as well."

John sat, and Bill noticed Darla tap her cheek. Agent Garcia removed his sunglasses.

Bill asked, "How can I help you?"

Garcia replied, "We're here to help you. Dr. Adam Klein called Dr. Joshua Zeev. I believe you're familiar with their names."

Bill nodded.

Garcia continued. "Joshua is currently in protective custody. I'm afraid I can't disclose more than that. When Dr. Zeev explained to us the urgency in finding you, we flew him up here so the two of you could meet."

Bill looked towards the front door. "Where is he?"

Darla responded, "He isn't in the car. We need to take you to him."

John interrupted, "How did you find us? Did you speak to my wife?"

Darla said, "We tried, but she wouldn't tell us where you were. You have a very protective spouse."

John answered, "She's the best."

Garcia said, "Yes. Well, fortunately, we had Bill's phone number. I tracked the location of his phone."

Bill asked, "Is that legal?"

Darla's eyes seemed to penetrate Bill's soul, and something inside him told him not to ask that again.

Darla answered, "We have a wide latitude with this case."

Both agents stood up, and Garcia said, "Please, both of you, pack up. We need to leave. If I thought to track your phone, others might try as well."

Bill and John asked, "Who?"

Garcia answered, "It's need to know. Mr. Palazzo, we don't believe you are in any sort of danger, but I think you should go back home, just in case. We'll leave an agent in the area to watch this house for a couple of days. If things change, we'll be in touch."

Bill asked, "What about me?"

Darla answered, "You're coming with us."

Bill folded his arms across his chest. "I'm not sure I like the way that sounds."

Garcia answered, "We're taking you to Joshua."

Bill nodded and walked briskly towards the bedroom. He could hear John exchange words with the agents and then hurry upstairs. In a few minutes, he had everything tossed hastily into his suitcase and zippered it closed with some effort.

Bill returned to the agents with his suitcase.

Darla said, "Let's go."

Bill put up his finger and hollered from the bottom of the stairs. "Do I need to help with anything?"

John poked his head out from the upstairs bedroom and said, "I've got it. Let me know that you're safe wherever you end up."

Bill nodded and then followed the agents outside. A black SUV with tinted windows sat at the entrance of the driveway. Bill noticed a black sedan with a man standing next to it in the house's lower driveway.

Bill pointed, "Who's that?"

Garcia answered, "Frank. He'll keep an eye on things. Please, we need to leave."

They loaded his suitcase and put Bill in the back seat. The two agents slipped inside the front seats, put on their sunglasses, and were driving down highway twenty-one in a couple of short minutes.

Bill asked, "So, where are we going?"

Darla answered, "You'll see soon enough."

Bill's cell phone rang. He pulled it from his pocket and asked, "May I answer it?"

Darla turned to face him. "Please don't say where you're going."

"That won't be hard, I don't have a clue."

Carol's voice was shrill on the other end, "Are you working with the CIA?"

Bill stammered, "Wait, what?"

Darla turned back to Bill and said, "Please ask Ms. Lewis not to shoot our agent."

Carol sounded insistent. "There's a Frank Jones at your door. He claims he's with the CIA. Do you know about this?"

Bill asked, "Why are you at my house? I thought you'd be at work."

Carol answered, "I got laid off, so I thought I'd come over and check on things. Five minutes after I got here, some guy in sunglasses is telling me he's CIA, and I have to leave."

Bill said, "Hang on."

He covered the receiver and asked Darla and Garcia, "How'd you know she'd be there.'

Garcia said, "Please,"

Darla interrupted, "Remember, CIA. We've been keeping track of Ms. Lewis since the attack. She was an early person of interest, but we cleared her."

Bill's eyes widened, "Person of interest? My admin?"

Darla turned and faced the front.

Carol's voice sounded irritated, "Don't put me on hold. I'm debating whether or not to shoot this guy."

Bill's voice rose an octave, "You have a gun?"

"Baby, I'm a black woman in the south, of course, I have a gun. Don't worry, it's legal."

Bill took and deep breath and said, "He's CIA. It's about the office shooting. Please do what he asks."

Carol's voice grew quiet, "Are you in some kind of trouble?"

Bill answered, "No."

"Are we in danger?" asked Carol.

Bill answered honestly, "Not if we listen to them."

Carol sounded calmer. "Alright. You better call me later and tell me what's going on."

Bill replied, "When I figure it out myself, you'll be the first to know."

"Don't make me call you," warned Carol.

"I won't. I need to go."

Bill hung up the phone. He looked out the window and noticed them passing the only Walmart in town. The car made a left on to highway four-twenty-one business, and they were soon puttering through downtown North Wilkesboro. Bill spoke up as the vehicle turned left on highway eighteen.

"We're headed to the airport?"

Darla turned towards Bill. The surprise on her face lasted only a second. "How do you know that?"

Bill shrugged, "It makes sense. You said you flew here."

Darla and Garcia looked at each other. Garcia asked, "Do a lot of people use this airport?"

"I don't know. It's not like it's Charlotte Douglas."

Darla's posture relaxed, and the three sat in silence as they approached the airport. Bill could feel a knot forming in his stomach. He wiped his palms on his slacks as the SUV slowly made its way through the hangers. They pulled up next to a Honda Jet.

Bill asked, "Is he in the plane?"

Neither agent said a word. They exited the vehicle, and Garcia opened Bill's door. Bill got out of the car.

Garcia pointed at the hanger's small door, "Joshua's in there. Darla will join you. I have an old friend to visit."

"Who?" asked Bill.

"It's need to know, and you don't need to know."

Bill stepped around the vehicle next to Darla, and Garcia got in and drove away.

Darla asked, "Nervous?"

"Yea. I don't know. None of this makes sense."

Darla placed her hand gently on Bill's back, "Don't worry. Joshua is one of the best men I've known. He'll help you sort this out."

Bill stood there. Darla pressed harder against his back, and he started making his way towards the closed door.

CHAPTER 11

The steel handle felt cold against Bill's hand. Darla stood behind and waited for him to enter. Bill took a deep breath, heard the bolt give way with a click, and pushed inward. For a moment, everything seemed covered by shadows as his eyes adjusted. Only one of the lights at the top of the hanger was on. The building sat empty except for some tool chests near the hanger's rear.

Bill looked to his left, and four feet away stood a man in dark sunglasses and a suit with a submachine gun. He kept it diagonally pointed to the ground. At the far end of the building sat a man behind a folding table. He stood, and Bill took a deep breath and stayed his ground.

Darla gently pushed him in further and entered the hanger, shutting the door.

Darla said, "Follow me."

Bill fell in line behind Darla, and the man began to walk towards them. Bill could see immediately that he was the same height. As his face came into view, Bill held his breath. He looked like the Joshua in his dreams. Gray hair and deep lines in his brow made the man look older, wiser. Something clicked inside of Bill. He walked briskly past Darla.

"Joshua," Bill said with the excitement of a small child.

Joshua held out his arms, and the two embraced. Bill could feel the tears from Joshua's face, and for some reason, he was crying too. He still held no memories beyond his dreams, but it felt like he had found a long-lost family member.

The two let go, and Joshua patted Bill's shoulders. "Look at you. You've turned into such a fine young man."

Darla walked up, "I can see I don't have to make introductions. I know you two have a lot to talk about. Frank and I will be over by the door."

Joshua put his arm around Bill, "Come, my boy. We have much to discuss."

He led Bill over to the table, and the two men sat down. Joshua's eyes twinkled with delight.

Bill looked at the armed guard, then back at Joshua and asked, "Who are you?"

Joshua answered, "I thought you recognized me."

"I feel like I know you, but I've only seen your face in my dreams."

Joshua leaned forward, "What did I look like?"

"Younger."

Joshua grinned. "Yes. We were both much younger then."

Bill asked again, "Who are you?"

The smile left Joshua's face, "I can answer all your questions, but I'm going to need you to trust me."

Bill looked over his shoulder at Darla and the guard conversing quietly by the door. The hanger had many shadows, and Bill hoped someone was not hiding in one of them.

Bill looked back at Joshua, "What do you have in mind?"

Joshua pulled a gold pen out of his pocket, angled it so it caught what little light was in the room, and began to twirl it. He asked, "Do you remember this pen?"

Bill stared hard at the object. "It feels familiar."

"Keep watching it, and just relax. Your memories will start to come back."

Bill watched it for a few more seconds. He blinked and shook his head. "Hey, you're making me drowsy."

Joshua's voice sounded a little distant. "That's just your brain, remembering. Focus on the pen and let your eyelids relax. Do you remember the woods we used to walk in?"

Bill thought he could see a green forest around him. His eyes opened slightly, and the glint of the cold pen caught his eyes.

Joshua spoke softly, "You do remember."

Bill mumbled, "Yes."

Joshua's voice drew Bill in. "Good. Do you want to go there together?"

Bill asked, "Why?"

"To find your answers."

Bill nodded and smiled, "Hurry, Joshua, let's go now."

Joshua's voice was soothing. "Okay, let's go on an adventure. Do you see the woods?"

The forest came into focus. Trees created a canopy above, and crisp air felt good against Bill's bare chest. Joshua walked beside him. Both wore wolfskin, but Joshua also had a shirt on.

Joshua turned and asked, "Do you know where we are?"

Bill answered, "Helvsgud."

"That's close enough. We have a short walk this way."

The two walked in silence. Bill breathed in the fresh air and beat his chest. "It's good to be home."

Joshua said nothing. They broke through the edge of the woods and into the clearing. Farmers were tending their crops, and people were walking to and fro through the village gate. Joshua sat down in front of a thatched hut and invited Bill to join him.

Joshua said, "I want you to concentrate on me. Tell me the last time you were in the village."

Bill's brow wrinkled. He drew in his breath. "The farms, they were on fire."

"It's okay, Bill. There're no fires now. Why were they on fire?"

Bill answered, "Raiders, they came to attack the village."

Joshua asked in a soft voice, "What happened?"

Bill continued, "I protected the village. I went berserk and saved the town, except." Bill's voice trailed off.

"Except what?"

Bill said, "Lori," and then began to weep.

Joshua held Bill as he cried. Bill finally wiggled free and growled, "I need to find her killer."

"I thought you killed the raiders?"

Bill answered, "I did, but there's someone else."

Joshua's whispered, "Who told you that?"

Bill looked Joshua in the eye, "King Adam told me. He said dangerous men were after you and my brother. Perhaps they are after me too."

A strange voice echoed in the wind, "Doctor, we have company coming."

Joshua spoke faster, "Bill, we have to leave now, but we will come back. I want you to remember everything we have talked about."

Bill nodded.

Joshua continued, "Listen to me. We need to leave the village. Come back with me to the hanger. Will you do that."

Bill nodded again.

Joshua continued, "Okay, I'm going to count to three. When you open your eyes, we will both be back in the hanger with Darla and Frank. One, Two, Three."

Bill opened his eyes, blinked, and found himself back inside the hanger. Darla was walking quickly in their direction.

She said, "Our perimeter confirmed a vehicle coming in this direction with two men. They don't appear friendly."

"What about Garcia?"

Darla hollered over her shoulder, "Too far."

Joshua asked, "What do you want us to do?"

Darla pointed to a rolling tool chest a few feet away. "Get behind that. I'll tell you when you can come out." She hollered across the hanger. "Frank, I'll take this back door."

Frank answered, "Heard."

Bill whispered to Joshua, "I can help."

Joshua put his hand on Bill's shoulder, "Stay here. Darla and Frank are more than capable of handling two men."

Frank peeked out the front door, shut it, and hollered, "They're here."

Darla yelled out, "Nobody move, make them come to us."

Bill spoke to Joshua, "Come to us? Is she crazy?"

Darla answered, "Bill, sound carries in here, remember that. We want them inside because they could have a sniper. Our people on the perimeter will secure the outside once these two come inside."

Darla's radio squawked, "I only have eyes on one, but both have left the vehicle."

The front door burst open, and machine-gun fire raked the hanger. Bill watched Darla dive down and flip over the table for cover. His heart started to beat louder. Joshua put a gentle hand back on his shoulder and whispered, "Stay calm. They know what they're doing."

Bill took two deep breaths. His heart still beat loudly but slowed slightly. The back door slammed against the metal wall and echoed through the hanger. The gunfire stopped. Bill ignored Joshua tugging on his shirt, and peaked over the tool chests. A masked man had his arm around Darla with a gun to her head. On the other side of the hanger, Frank's gun was pointed at his partner.

The masked man yelled across to Frank, "Let my partner go, and she lives. We only want Bill."

Frank's gun went off, and the side of the stranger's head exploded as he fell to the ground.

The masked assailant holding Darla yelled, "Morons!"

Bill's heartbeat grew louder and faster. He looked at Darla with the gun to her head and the masked man saying something in her ear he could not make out. The captor slipped his hand off the finger guard and rested it on the trigger. Bill's world turned crimson.

His howl shook the metal walls of the hanger.

Darla yelled, "No!"

Bill growled, "No."

He grabbed the top half of the tool chest. The masked man pointed his gun in Bill's direction, and Darla's elbow collided with the man's ribs. His weapon shot wild before falling to the ground. Bill released the heavy tool chest towards his would-be killer, and Darla dove to the ground.

The fully loaded tool cabinet collided with the man's head. The cabinet's momentum carried the man to the ground and crushed his skull between the tool chest and the concrete. Bill smiled, doubled over, and tried to catch his breath.

Darla yelled, "You idiot."

The sound of Darla's voice caused Bill to look up. To his surprise, she was marching at a brisk pace in his direction.

Darla continued to rant, "You just killed our only lead. Who told you to do that? Was it you, Joshua?"

Joshua slowly emerged, shaking his head.

Bill took in large gulps of air and tried to regain his strength. "I was trying to save you."

Darla walked up, grabbed Bill by the shirt, and stood him up.

Fire flashed in her eyes, "Get this straight. I'm a big girl and can handle myself. Unless I ask for help, stay out of my way."

Bill stammered, "But he had a gun to your head."

Darla poked him in the chest, and he back-peddled. His weakened legs gave way, and he fell on his butt on the concrete floor. Darla glared down at him, "I had it under control."

Frank walked up and extended a hand. Bill took it and was helped to his feet.

Frank said, "Bill, that guy didn't want to die. He was hiding behind Darla. The perp didn't care that I shot his partner. All he wanted to do was negotiate his way to the back door. He would have rolled in an instant."

Darla broke in, "At least he would have before you made a pancake of his skull."

Frank went over to check the dead man's pockets. He looked up at Darla, "Nothing, just like his buddy over there."

Joshua spoke up, "How did they find us?"

Darla turned and kicked the dead man's legs. "I screwed up.

"Bill."

Bill quickly replied, "Yes, ma'am."

"My name is Darla."

Bill stammered, "I'm sorry, it's just, well, it's just how we were raised."

Darla asked, "Do you always say yes, sir and ma'am?"

"Yes, ma'am."

Darla waved him off, "Whatever, I don't have time for this. Give me your cell phone."

"Why?"

Darla stuck out her hand, "Give it to me, or I'll take it."

Bill handed Darla his cell. She threw it on the ground on stomped on his until it lay in pieces and its broken screen went black. She picked it up and handed it to Bill.

Darla said, "Now it's secure."

Joshua asked, "I wonder how long they've been tracking Bill?"

Darla answered, "Long enough to create this fiasco. We're compromised people, everyone on the plane."

Bill asked, "What about me?"

Darla answered, "I said, everyone."

Joshua spoke up, "You'll like where we're going."

"What if I say no?"

Frank waved around, "Then their friends are coming to find you, and I don't think they'll care if you're dead or alive."

Bill nodded and then asked, "What about my house and my friends?"

Darla sounded irritated, "We'll talk about it on the plane."

She dialed a number, and her team gathered their things. She said, "We've been compromised. I need a cleanup team here, stat. Tell Alice that we're headed back home, and Bill's coming with us."

Darla quickly hung up and grabbed the walkie talkie. "Are we secure outside?"

A voice answered, "Roger."

Darla spoke into the mic, "Okay, wait for the cleanup team."

"Roger."

Darla commanded the group, "Quickly, to the plane."

The crew briskly got into the plane. Darla took the front left seat, and Frank took the right. Joshua and Bill sat across from each other. In less than three minutes, she had the plane airborne. After another twenty minutes, Darla left the cockpit and sat down with Joshua and Bill.

She said, "Look, I'm sorry I was so harsh. Adrenaline and all that."

Bill answered, "I understand, but you need to understand that my world is upside down. I've lost my fiancée. Someone is trying to kill me. Suddenly, the CIA is taking me to a secret location with a man I barely remember who did something to my head because of this monster inside me."

Joshua spoke up, "We had hoped our reunion would be smoother."

Darla said, "We'll be at our island soon. You'll meet my husband, your brother."

"Harold's married? To you?"

Darla's brow wrinkled, "Yes, why?"

"It never made the papers."

Darla asked, "Why should it?"

"Well, the business rags keep up with something like that."

Darla said, "We've had to stay below the radar. Anyway, you'll meet Harold and the rest of the gang. I think you'll find your accommodations acceptable."

Joshua spoke up, "Once you settle in, we can continue bringing back your memories and help you understand who you are."

Bill asked, "What about the people coming after us?"

Darla answered, "Don't worry about that. That's my job. Your job is to listen to Joshua."

Bill looked out the window and muttered, "It doesn't look like I have a choice."

CHAPTER 12

The small jet was much like the pictures Bill had seen in brochures. White stitched leather covered the chairs. A small bathroom was wedged in the back of the cabin. The airport's tension was behind him, but Bill's body remained taut as he huddled close to Joshua, who sat opposite of him.

Bill said, "Let me get this straight. A brother I don't remember signed on with the CIA because his father's friend betrayed their family, caused his parents' deaths, and decimated the company."

"Yes."

Bill continued, "After that, Harold agreed to work with the CIA to save his father's company. However, a sting Harold was involved in failed because a tracking circuit designed by some CIA engineer blew their cover."

Joshua nodded.

"Now, this guy is after the CIA operative, right?"

Joshua answered, "That about covers it."

Bill raised his eyebrows, "How do you figure? Why would this guy care about any of us? I thought you said he credited Harold and Darla with saving his life once. Why would he come after me? Harold and I don't even know each other."

"You said you think he called you when you were living in uptown Charlotte. Did he believe you when you said you didn't know Harold?"

"The guy didn't sound as if he cared. It was like he was trying to convince me that it was a fact more than fish for information. I thought it was a scam."

Joshua answered, "Possibly."

Bill asked, "Besides, you and Darla were back in the warehouse. Why didn't they grab one of you? Those guys asked for me."

Joshua shrugged, "I'm afraid you'll have to ask Darla. That's a question for the CIA."

Bill sat up and looked out over the teal waters of the Caribbean. The shadow of coral, sharks and other objects appeared through the clear water.

He looked back and to Joshua and raised his voice, "How much longer?"

Joshua looked out the window, "Oh, we should be landing very soon."

"Where are we?"

Joshua answered, "I'm afraid I never figured that out. Harold and Darla say it's outside U.S. waters. Harold owns his own little country, in a sense."

"So, my brother is a king and a Chairman of the board?"

Joshua smiled, "Something like that."

Frank turned around from the cockpit and hollered, "Buckle up, we're ready to land."

Bill noticed Joshua tightened his seatbelt, so he followed suit. Joshua's knuckles were white as the plane descended closer to the water. Bill's seat faced the rear of the plane. The jet slowed, and an alarm sounded intermittently from the cockpit. Each time it clanged, the engines increased and then decreased again. The aircraft was so low that Bill was afraid they would hit the water.

He barely caught a glimpse of the runway extending out into the ocean when the wheels firmly planted on the asphalt. For a moment, his back was pressed hard into the seat, unable to move. The brakes released, and they slowly rolled several feet before pulling to the side.

The two men unbuckled, and Darla appeared from the cockpit.

She looked over at Joshua, "I hope that wasn't too dramatic."

Bill asked Joshua, "You don't like to fly."

"I don't like small planes. Darla, you did an excellent job as usual."

Frank hollered from inside the cockpit, "I heard that. You're going to hurt my feelings."

Joshua answered, "It's alright, Frank. You're a close second."

The three gave a short laugh, and Bill stretched his arms and touched both sides of the cabin.

Joshua turned to Bill, "Please, wait here for a moment. I don't know if Harold knows you're on board."

Darla spoke up, "Trust me, he knows."

Joshua nodded once, "Well then, it's time to meet your brother."

Frank remained in the cockpit, checking instruments and writing in the log. Darla opened the door and led the way. Next came Joshua. Bill walked to the opened door, and his eyes grew wide.

Two men with sub-machine guns stood a few yards away. A young Hispanic woman barreled into Joshua and squeezed his waist until his face was crimson. Darla embraced a large man who was standing just beyond the stairs. Bill was shocked at how different Harold looked in person than his business magazine photos.

His red hair was no longer professionally styled, and he had grown a furry, red beard. Bill thought the man resembled a lion. A warm breeze hit Bill in the face, and his flannel shirt and jeans that were so comfortable a few hours ago in the mountains only added to the sweat from his nerves.

Bill made his way down the short steps, and Harold walked briskly in his direction. Bill extended his hand, and Harold caught him up in a tight embrace and lifted his feet off the ground. Bill could feel his face flush for what felt like several seconds.

Harold finally put him down and said, "I've waited for this moment my whole life."

Pain emanated from Bill's side. He rolled up his sleeves as sweat dripped off his forehead.

Harold asked, "Well, what about you?"

Bill cleared his throat awkwardly, "I'm sorry, I'm not sure what to say. I didn't know I had a brother until today."

Harold's eyes narrowed, and his gaze dropped to the asphalt.

Darla stepped forward and spoke up. "Honey, Chuck's men gave us a sendoff."

He looked up and grabbed Darla's arm, "What? Are you alright?"

Darla nodded, "Bill made sure of it. I'm afraid he's as protective as you. I didn't have any suspects to interrogate."

Harold turned back to Bill, and a broad smile poked out from his bushy face. "Oh, you took out the bad guy?"

Bill shrugged, "Something like that."

Harold gave him a light punch on the shoulder, "I appreciate that, even if my wife doesn't. It seems the CIA teaches their agents that it's worth taking a bullet just to gather information."

Bill looked down, "I'd rather not talk about it."

Harold whispered, "First time?"

Bill shook his head sadly, and his shoulders sagged.

Harold spoke softly, "I understand. We'll talk later."

Joshua spoke up, "Why don't I show Bill to his bungalow."

"Bungalow?" asked Harold. "I don't think so. Bill can stay in the main house."

Bill raised his hand, "Do I get a say in this?"

Harold answered, "Of course."

Bill responded, "If it's all the same to you, I'd like to stay near Joshua, at least for now."

Harold took a step back, "Then the bungalow it is. Joshua will show you around. I would be honored if you'd join Darla and me for dinner. Joshua, you and Maria are invited as always."

The Hispanic woman Bill noticed earlier walked up and inserted herself between Harold and Bill. "I guess you didn't notice me. Boys have no manners. I'm Maria Zeev, Joshua's wife."

The twinkle in her eyes made Bill smile. She opened her arms, and Bill gave her a hug. Something was inviting about Maria. For a moment, Bill could imagine himself in his mother's arms, if he had had a mother.

She released him. "Joshua and I will take you to where you'll be staying."

Harold stuck out his hand and shook Bill's. "I'm so glad we're finally together. We'll talk more at dinner."

He and Darla grabbed an empty jeep and drove away. Joshua directed Bill to another jeep, and they all piled in. Maria took the driver's seat and then turned to Bill and asked, "Did you bring a change of clothes?"

Bill answered, "Just what I have on my back. We had to leave in a hurry."

Joshua answered, "I'm afraid Chuck's men insisted."

Maria pursed her lips and then asked Bill, "Was there shooting?"

Bill nodded.

Maria slugged Joshua in the arm. "I told you. You see, you shouldn't go on these missions. There's always shooting."

Joshua rubbed his shoulder, "We were perfectly safe."

Maria fired off a tirade in Spanish that Bill couldn't understand, but it was not pleasant judging from her tone. Joshua grimaced. She turned, started the vehicle, and spun the wheels as they headed away from the airstrip.

Maria eased off the gas pedal as they turned a corner. Joshua pointed over towards a narrow road, "Over there is the pier and fishing boat. Do you do any fishing?"

"What Carolina boy doesn't?" answered Bill.

"Ever do any ocean fishing?"

Bill answered, "Only up in new England."

Joshua said, "Good, we'll have to go out. Harold's a big fisherman too."

"From the looks of him, Harold is a big everything."

The three laughed as Maria stopped the jeep between a two-story bungalow with a huge front porch and a single-story building.

Maria said, "This is where we get out."

Joshua asked, "Maria, do you mind if I take Bill by myself to his bungalow?"

Maria answered, "Okay. I need to call Frank and see if we can get Bill some clothes. In the meantime, I'll pick out a couple of things from your closet. You two are about the same size."

Joshua nodded.

Bill said, "Thanks."

The two men entered the building. Joshua pointed around the open floor plan, "There isn't much to it. A kitchen over there, and you're in the great room. Through those sliding doors are the master bedroom and bathroom. I hope you like marble because the master bathroom is covered in it."

Bill responded, "Harold didn't strike me as the marble type."

"It was the previous owner."

Bill asked, "Anyone I've heard about?"

Joshua walked towards the front door, "He's dead, so it doesn't matter. Let's just say this place was like Epstein's island before he made the news."

Bill crossed his arms, "I hope you cleaned the place up."

Joshua chuckled, "Cleaned and sterilized. Check the place out, and when you feel up to it, come on over, and we'll talk for a little while."

"Sounds good."

Joshua left, and Bill walked over and looked inside the refrigerator. To his surprise, it appeared to be freshly stocked with Juice, Milk, meats, cheese, and every other staple he could think of. He checked the cabinets, and in addition to glasses, plates, and utensils, he found a fully stocked spice rack. Bill stretched and made his way into the bedroom.

The king-size bed looked comfortable, and the cold breeze coming from the air conditioner made him feel sleepy. He peeked inside the bathroom. Marble covered the jacuzzi garden tub, standalone shower, and even the sink pedestal. Bill rolled his eyes and then walked over and laid down on the bed.

He yawned and reached for his phone to call Carol. Bill stopped himself, rolled over on his back, and slapped the bed.

He looked up at the ceiling and said, "Of course, she crushed my phone. I guess I'm a bird in a gilded cage."

Bill closed his eyes for a moment. His breathing soon slowed. After a few minutes, his eyes began to twitch underneath his eyelids, and his breathing became shallow.

Chapter 13

Dust hung in the air and floated across the sunbeams peeking through the large exhaust hole of the longhouse roof. The smell of old leather, hay, and wet wood permeated the air. Bill stood up and paced by the smoldering firepit. Acrid smoke made his nose twitch.

The large hall's wooden benches could easily seat twenty. Yet, it felt abandoned as Bill paced up and down alone. He tried the two doors, and both were locked. Bill started to beat against them, but he'd been here before and knew it was useless.

He heard a noise to turned to face it. Joshua stood there in his wolfskin, but he was unarmed. Bill rushed over to him and stood just inches from his face.

"Is this you? Have you locked me away again? You can't do this."

Joshua shook his head once, "This is a memory."

Bill answered, "I remember falling asleep. Are you in the room with me?"

Joshua said, "No."

"Then why can't I get out?"

Joshua walked over and sat down and patted the wooden bench, "Come, sit."

Bill raised his arms and opened his mouth to protest, but then dropped his arms and joined Joshua.

Bill asked, "What's going on?"

Joshua turned to him. The compassion in his eyes almost made Bill weep. "You still feel guilty about breaking that boy's arm when you were a child."

Bill stood up, turned, and looked down at Joshua, "What? Are you serious? I've killed five men in like a week. I missed my fiancée's funeral because I was too ashamed to face her parents, and you think I care about breaking a kid's arm when I was a little?"

Joshua looked up at him, "This is a memory, a dream."

Bill flapped his arms and briskly walked in circles. "Great, it's a dream. I'm talking to myself while I'm sleeping."

"Bill."

Bill turned, but Joshua was no longer in the longhouse. He heard his voice again, "Bill."

Bill spun around again and again. He could hear Joshua's voice but could no longer see him.

"Bill, wake up."

Bill felt his body rocking and opened his eyes. Joshua stood over him. Grayer, smaller, in a flowered shirt with khaki shorts and a healthy tan.

Bill blinked twice, "Sorry, I must have been dreaming."

Joshua responded, "Why don't you come over to my place and let's talk."

Bill sat up on the edge of his bed. "Do you mean talk, or are you going to probe my mind again?"

"Just talk."

"Right. From one nightmare to the next."

"Nightmare?" asked Joshua.

"Forget it," responded Bill. "I'll be over in a couple of minutes after I freshen up."

Bill rubbed his face and ran his fingers through his hair as he stumbled towards the marbled bathroom. He grimaced at the cold marble against his feet. After he splashed cold water on his face he made his way out the front door and over to Joshua's.

Bill rocked in the large white wooden rocker. The porch and chair moaned in harmony beneath the seat as salt breezes awakened his senses. Birds he had not heard before called out in the overgrowth out of sight on the island. He could feel the ocean, although it was unseen and quiet. The sun's warmth gently blanketed the island.

Joshua asked, "Beautiful, isn't it?"

"I can see why Harold likes living here."

"Harold loves the ocean, but he would sell this place if he could. The island is not his style."

Bill's eyebrows went up. "He doesn't like it? How can you not enjoy such a beautiful piece of real estate?"

Joshua looked down and said, "The cost was higher than it was worth." He looked back up at Bill, "But that's Harold's story. Tell me, how are you doing?"

The front door opened, and Maria appeared, "I'm afraid my husband is a terrible host. Do you boys want anything to drink?"

Joshua took Maria's hand and kissed it. "I'd like one of my beers."

"I'd take some sweet tea if you have it."

Maria rolled her eyes, "What is it with putting sugar into iced tea. It's the only kind Joshua drinks too. Fortunately, I just made some."

Joshua chimed in, "Are you sure you don't want a beer?"

"Maybe with dinner."

Maria took her hand from Joshua and said, "I'll be back."

Joshua continued, "You've been through a lot recently. The loss of your family, killing those men. Darla told me about your job."

Bill asked, "How did she know?"

Joshua shrug, "They're CIA. I've learned not to ask because nobody tells you those sorts of things unless they get backed into a corner."

"Alright. Darla was upset over the man I killed today."

Joshua asked, "How does that make you feel?"

Bill scowled, "Really? You're using pop psychology? From everything I've been hearing, I thought you were smarter than that."

Maria came out, placed the drinks on the table, kissed Joshua's forehead, and went back inside. Joshua took a long sip from his bottle, and Bill finished half his glass of tea.

Joshua finally answered, "It's not pop psychology. I want to know how you are feeling, or thinking if you like. You couldn't have known what that man would do to Darla. If I had your ability, I would have done the same thing. If I'm honest, I felt helpless during the shootout."

Bill's eyes widened, "Really?"

Joshua answered, "Absolutely. Darla is a dear friend. What you did today was brave and good. You just met her, and you were willing to put yourself in danger to rescue her. We need more, not less of that in the world."

Bill finished his tea and then confessed, "But there's more to it. When I get into a rage, I enjoy killing whoever is in my path. It's like it can't wait to give them what they deserve."

"Afterwards, do you still feel good about it?"

Bill looked down and shook his head, "No. I feel guilty."

"Good."

Bill looked up, "Good?"

"I don't mean that's it's good you feel guilty. You shouldn't, but your guilt is a sign of regret. It means you're human, Bill. Why do you think so many military people have mental problems? We aren't designed to do violence. It's a learned behavior. Your first fight at the orphanage was with a boy who had been bullied when he was younger. Violence breeds violence, and its fruit is regret, guilt, and bitterness."

Bill asked, "Then what can I do? I can't hide what I am. We already tried that."

Joshua took Bill's hand, "Do you remember what you learned in church?"

"Do you mean about forgiveness in Jesus and all that religious stuff?"

Joshua let go of his hand and looked at him straight in the eye. "It isn't religious stuff. If you can accept there is a higher power, and he has given you a path to forgiveness, you can start forgiving yourself."

Bill's eyebrows narrowed, "But what if there isn't a higher power?"

"Then why do you feel guilty? If there isn't something more to the universe than your short time on earth, you can make your own rules based on your circumstances.

However, that guilt you feel doesn't come from you, and you know it. Think about that."

Joshua turned away and took a sip of his beer. Bill closed his eyes and listened to a warbler singing in the breeze.

Bill opened his eyes and ask Joshua, "Can we change subjects for a moment?"

"Sure."

Bill asked, "Why are these people after Harold?"

"Like I said on the plane, they aren't after Harold; they're after Garcia."

"Then why are they interested in me?"

Maria came out the front door with a pile of clothes in her arms.

She said, "Take these until Frank can get you some from the Keys."

Bill stood and relieved her of her load, "Thank you."

Maria continued, "Go get changed. We'll be going to dinner soon, and you should get out of those hot clothes."

Joshua spoke up, "We'll talk more later."

"Okay."

Bill headed back to his bungalow. Once inside, he looked up at the ceiling. "Well, where are you? You make me kill again and send me into hiding? How can any sort of God do such a thing? They said in church that you're good. Our preacher told us you made us, you made me. Well, what's good about any of this? Why would you make a killer? I ask for answers and you give me more misery. I seek knowledge and you show me a surrogate aunt and uncle. My heart feels black from despair and all I get is more violence. If you exist, where are you?"

CHAPTER 14

Bill stopped at the large mahogany door. Italian, French, and other influences created a beautiful and unique first impression of the sprawling home. The stucco and red tiled roof reminded Bill of his time in the California Wine Country.

Joshua asked, "Are you alright?"

"Yea. I'm getting an impression of Harold by his taste in houses."

Maria spoke up, "Harold didn't build this. He has better tastes than that. This was built by an evil man."

Bill asked, "Then why did Harold buy it?"

Maria answered, "The government gave it to him."

"Gave it?"

Joshua interrupted, "Perhaps we should go inside. I'm sure Harold will be happy to tell you more when the time is right. Please, keep my wife's words in mind; this is not what your brother is about."

Joshua opened the door, and Bill hesitated.

"Come on," insisted Joshua.

Bill followed them through the marbled entryway and into the parlor. Inside sat inviting overstuffed cream-colored couches and chairs.

Just beyond the parlor, a retractable wall stood opened. Harold and Darla stood near two pillars with drinks in their hands, talking. As soon as Harold caught sight of the group, he quickly approached them, weaving his way past Joshua and Maria and straight to Bill.

"Welcome to my home, such as it is. I apologize for the décor. I'm afraid it mostly came this way."

Bill shook his hand, "Thank you. Joshua and I were just discussing the house."

"It isn't really me, but Garcia and Darla say we're safe here, and we're outside jurisdictional waters, so I'm my own little country."

"Convenient."

Harold chuckled, "It does have its tax perks. Would you like a drink?"

"What are you having?"

Harold answered, "It's a rum runner. It's sort of our drink of choice. Frank keeps the alcohol low and the fruit juice high."

"Do you have any beer?"

Joshua spoke up, "Let me have Frank get you a Copper."

Bill's eyebrows went up. "You get Olde Mecklenburg here in the kingdom of Harold?"

Joshua smiled, "It's the only privilege I requested."

Bill raised his hand, "Sign me up."

Joshua excused himself and headed over to talk with a man behind the bar next to the pool. Maria, Harold, and Bill joined Darla.

Bill asked, "Why are so many of your servants and guards named Frank?"

Darla answered, "Oh, they don't work for us. They work for the U.S. government. They're part of the CIA detail."

"The CIA renames all their agents Frank?"

Darla smiled, looked at Harold, and then back at Bill. "We use different names. These are some of our best agents, so they must use an alias. We decided to call everyone Frank because it's easier to remember. It also gives us an additional layer of security. If you ever meet anyone claiming to be from Harold's residence and he doesn't call himself Frank, you'll know he's lying."

"Why aren't there any female agents?"

Darla answered, "I believe I'm offended."

Bill shook his head, "I meant besides you."

Harold spoke up, "I don't need another woman on the island."

Darla responded, "Not if you know what's good for you. Besides, we have Maria."

Bill turned to Maria, "You're CIA?"

Maria scowled, "No."

Darla wrapped her arm around Maria's shoulder and pulled her petite frame close. "Maria is worth ten CIA agents. She's fearless, and she orders people around better than Alice."

Bill asked, "Who's Alice?"

Darla replied, "My boss. She's running this project. You'll meet her eventually."

Joshua brought over two glasses of beer and handed one to Bill. He took a long swallow and smiled. Maria pointed to her lip, and Bill wiped the foam from his mouth.

Bill asked, "So, what now?"

Darla answered, "Garcia will return tomorrow. We'll debrief each other and then decide our next steps. It's obvious Chuck is making his move to exact his revenge."

Harold pointed to the chairs, "Why don't we get comfortable."

Everyone sat. Harold took the chair at the front of the table and asked Bill to sit on his left side, and Joshua sat to Bill's left. Bill looked across the table at Darla. "Why do you guys think this is about revenge? Why come after me if it was about the CIA?"

"Chuck's a psychopath. He probably thinks grabbing you would pull us out of the woodwork. You saw what happened at the airport."

Bill nodded and took a sip of beer. Then he said, "Yea, but they weren't looking to kill everyone. You said yourself that the guy who took you hostage just wanted to get away. All they wanted was me. The only connection I have to anybody here is Harold and Joshua. If you ask me, they're after Harold."

Joshua spoke up, "Why do you think that?"

Bill shrugged, "I'm not a spy, but Harold's involved in nukes. Maybe this Chuck fella thinks he can get hold of some nuclear weapons if he gets hold of Harold."

Darla shook her head, "Chuck's not that dumb."

Harold spoke up, "Besides, he could have taken me at the beach."

"What beach?" asked Bill.

Darla jumped in. "When our sting went awry, Chuck had us pinned down with a machine gun. He commented about he and Harold being even and that he would get his revenge. That's why we think he's after the CIA team."

Bill scowled, "I don't understand. He could have killed everyone on the beach by the sounds of it."

Harold answered, "Yes, but Darla and I had saved his life before."

"Was anyone else on the beach?"

"Garcia," answered Darla. "Chuck had him pinned down."

Bill mumbled, "Something's missing."

Joshua patted Bill's shoulder, "It's nothing you need to worry about, my boy. Let Darla, Garcia, and the rest of the agents worry with Chuck. Once he's captured, we can leave our extended vacation, and they can figure out the rest."

The table was quiet as the group sipped their drinks.

Harold caught Bill's attention. "I hope you like to-night's menu. It's Rock House Store BBQ from Stallings with potato salad, bbq beans, and banana pudding."

Bill's eyes brightened. "Rock House Store? Out here? How?"

Darla answered, "Please, we're the CIA."

The table erupted with laughter, and Bill looked around confused.

Harold continued, "Sorry, it's an inside joke you'll discover soon enough. When my wife was researching your expenses, she discovered multiple BBQ restaurant purchases. I suggested we fly some in at my expense once I heard you were coming to the island. I hope I guessed right."

Bill's eyes glistened, "It was one of our favorite take-out's."

"Our?" asked Harold.

"Lori and me."

Harold nodded and whispered, "I'm sorry."

The food came out, and everyone dug in. The table was quiet for the next fifteen minutes as everyone enjoyed their meal.

Joshua finally spoke up, "I do miss home."

Bill nodded in approval.

Harold responded, "I think I've been missing out by living on the west coast."

Joshua asked Bill, "Is anyone watching your place while you're gone?"

Bill dropped his fork, and it clattered against the plate. He quickly wiped his mouth and said, "Oh shoot. I need to call Carol."

"Is she watching your house?" asked Joshua.

Bill answered, "Yes, and she was questioned by the CIA today. She said I better call, or she'd call me."

Joshua responded, "At least she hasn't called."

Bill looked over at Darla.

Darla said, "I'm afraid that's my fault. I had to destroy Bill's phone."

She reached for her phone and extended it to Bill. "Here, use mine. It's secure and can't be traced."

Bill dialed Carol's number. It rang several times and finally went to voicemail. "Hey, it's Bill. I'm fine, but my phone is broken. Call me back on this number, and I'll tell you what's going on."

Bill hung up the phone and handed it back to Darla.

Maria spoke up, "I think your friend is angry with you."

"Why?"

Maria answered, "Because you ignored her."

Joshua intervened, "Carol is his administrator, honey. Bill's fiancée was killed not too long ago."

Maria looked around Joshua at Bill, a tear ran down her cheek, "I'm sorry."

"Thank you," said Bill. He continued, "I'm sure Carol is just tied up. She's watching my house, her apartment. There are a hundred reasons she wouldn't answer. Now, where's that banana pudding?"

Frank left his location behind the bar and disappeared into the house. A few minutes later, he came out with a tray full of banana pudding in glass dessert cups. Everyone took one, and again silence ensued. A sigh of satisfaction bounced around the table in a round-robin fashion as each person finished off the remnants of their desert.

Darla's phone rang. She pulled it out of her pocket. "Agent Brown speaking."

There was a pause, and then Darla said, "Who?"

Another pause ensued, and Harold, Bill, Joshua, and Maria all looked at one another inquisitively.

Darla spoke once more, "If you hurt her." She stopped for a moment, "I want proof of life."

Darla extended the phone to Bill and said, "It's Chuck, he has Carol."

CHAPTER 15

A strange voice on the other end of the sound phone sounded chipper, "Billy, it's been a long time."

Bill scowled, "It's Bill. If you had ever spoken to me, you'd know that."

The stranger laughed, "Of course, I should have remembered."

"Who are you?"

"I'm wounded. You don't remember me. It's Chuck, Chuck McGill, but you can just call me Chuck."

Bill stood up and started to pace behind the others, "Why would I remember you?"

Chuck responded, "I called you when you were still in uptown Charlotte. It's a shame you sold that place, by the way."

Bill responded, annoyed, "I don't remember your call."

Chuck laughed, "I suspect not. You sounded distracted. I'm guessing you had a lady friend."

"My fiancée. You know, the one you had killed."

Chuck was quiet for a moment and then answered in a low voice, "Yes, I'm sorry about that. I told my men not to hurt anyone. I don't need the attention. Nigel was an idiot and a horrible accountant, but I was shorthanded."

Bill growled, "So that was you."

Chuck let out an audible sigh, "I can hear you have your brother's disposition. I can't blame you. I'd be looking for revenge myself. Unfortunately, we're past that."

"Past what?" asked Bill.

Chuck's voice became more assertive, "Past everything. You see, I want one thing, Harold."

"Why?" asked Bill.

Chuck answered, "I'm afraid that's need to know, and the less you know, the better."

Bill responded, "You sound like the CIA."

"Let's just say we share best practices."

Bill's free hand began to move around, and his pacing quickened, "I can't give you Harold. Why am I involved? Why did you involve Carol?"

"Leverage, my boy."

Bill stopped and growled, "I swear, if you kill her."

Chuck interrupted, "I would never kill such a beautiful woman. Here, see for yourself."

The phone line was quiet, and then Carol's familiar voice quaked through the receiver. "Bill, is that you?"

Bill's voice was anxious. "Are you alright?"

"He's got me guarded by sex traffickers. They keep telling me how much money they'll make off me. I swear, I'll die before I become a slave. Bill," the phone went silent.

"Carol!"

Chuck's voice responded, "You see, safe as can be."

Bill's heartbeat grew louder, "I swear, if anyone touches her, I'll find you and tear you apart."

Chuck's voice was calm, "That is entirely up to you and the CIA."

Bill was exasperated. "I don't have any pull here."

"I think you're not giving yourself enough credit. Your brother and his wife have plenty of pull, and I'm quite certain they'll see things your way."

"What if they don't?" asked Bill.

"Then I give Carol to my friends," answered Chuck menacingly.

Bill was urgent, "She'd rather die."

"That's up to her."

The phone line went dead. Bill squeezed the phone, and an audible crack caused Darla to yell, "Please, don't. It's the only link we have to Carol."

Bill stopped himself and handed the phone back to Darla. She looked it over and put it back in her pocket.

Bill said, "I need to go for a walk."

Harold answered, "Stay on the road and trails, and you should be okay."

Darla hollered, "Wait!"

Bill turned, "What?"

"What did Chuck say?"

Bill's brow wrinkled, "You know what he said."

"How would I know?"

Bill answered, "Because you needed to."

He turned and quickly walked through the opened wall, past the parlor, and was soon out the front door. He stopped on the front porch and debated heading back to his bungalow but instead went to his right and followed the driveway and shell covered lane to see where it would lead.

White LED lights sat at the edge of the foliage next to the road. Their pale white light clearly showed the path while not disturbing the night sky. Bill had not bothered to look up. He was too busy following the ground lights and blocking out everything but the eerie glow at his feet. His mindless trek stopped when he came to a fork in the road.

A lit footpath veered off to the right into the darkness. The shadows of shrubs, trees, and sawgrass sat in the distance. The other direction was the road and lights that led towards a small bend. Bill looked up for the first time and noticed the full moon. His eyes adjusted to the darkness, and he could make out the pale reflection on the plant life ahead.

He turned right and began to follow the path. An occasional rustle of leaves or limbs by an unseen animal or reptile would startle Bill, but he kept moving forward. Although the plants were cut back, a breeze would sometimes cover some of the pathway's lights. He was considering turning around when the world broke open before him.

A small beach lay nestled between the water and overgrowth. The same lights lined the back of the beach. The full moon reflected off the water, creating diamonds on its ripples. Small rocks dotted the muted white sand, and a large, flat boulder sat partway in the water. A wrought iron bench sat just to the right of the rock.

Bill sat down on the bench and looked skyward for the first time. A canopy of stars spread out before him. He smiled and remembered sneaking out at night after lights out at the orphanage. He would lay back on a picnic table in the quadrant and try to count the stars above his head. As he grew older, he would try and identify the clusters.

A frown formed on Bill's face. All the stars looked the same. Concentrating, Orion's belt began to peek out from among the stars, and then grew so obvious Bill wondered how he had missed it at all. A reddish orb, slightly larger than the rest, appeared to pulse.

Bill pointed up and said to no one, "Mars. You're Mars."

His forehead wrinkled, and his brow creased. Bill continued pointing to the sky and asked, "How can you do this." He raised both hands, "Look at this. How can you make all of this and let this world suffer so much?"

Bill dropped his hands sat silent. Only the breeze disturbed the plants behind him.

He spoke again, "Why? Why Lori? Why Carol? Why am I a killer? If you created me, if you created this, tell me why. Is that too much to ask?"

"Maybe it's above your paygrade."

Bill jumped at the sound of Harold's voice and sat up.

Harold continued, "Sorry, I wasn't trying to snoop."

Bill ran his hand through his hair, "Did you follow me?"

"No, this is where I come to think and pray."

Bill looked over at Harold's large silhouette as he walked towards him. He stood as Harold drew near. "I'm sorry, I didn't know this was your spot. I can leave."

Harold put his hand on Bill's shoulder, "Don't be silly. Stay."

"I can see why you come here."

Harold turned and faced the darkness and diamonds on the water. "Yes, this place has an effect on people." He turned back to Bill, "Please, sit down. Let me grab my chair."

Bill looked around for a chair when Harold climbed up on the flat rock. He crossed his legs and looked in

Bill's direction. Even by the moonlight, Bill could see Harold's eyes dance.

Bill asked, "What did you come here to think about?"

"Darla told me what Chuck wants."

"Let me guess, you're not going."

Harold stretched out his legs and leaned back on his arms. "Actually, I volunteered, but I was overruled by the CIA and my wife."

"Your wife works for the CIA."

"Exactly."

Bill stood up, "So, my friend dies because your wife is afraid something will happen to you."

Harold sat up and extended his hands, "Hold on. Don't get too far ahead of yourself. Darla promised me they'll get Carol back alive without giving me up."

Bill walked over and leaned against the rock, next to Harold. "You'll have to excuse me if I'm not convinced. Your wife seemed pretty surprised by the men showing up in the hanger. What's to stop her from being wrong again?"

Harold shrugged, "Nothing, I guess. But, I trust my wife, and I trust Maria. Neither woman would want any other woman to end up as a sex slave."

"So, is Maria some sort of spy expert?"

Harold answered, "No. She was sort of a house-keeper and a nanny to me growing up, almost like the big sister no boy ever wants. That doesn't sound like much, but don't let her humble background fool you. Her family came to our country to escape the cartel in Mexico. She saw some horrible things growing up. She understands what Carol is facing. If she trusts Darla and Garcia to get her out, I do too."

"After talking with Chuck, I'm convinced I was right," said Bill. "You were the target the whole time. But why?"

Harold leaned back again. "I wish I knew what's so interesting about me. Chuck had his chances earlier to take me. I'm not sure what's changed."

Bill sighed, "So, Lori died for this?"

"Not just Lori, but maybe my parents too. I least I think they did."

"You're not sure?"

Harold shook his head. "John Richmond was a close friend of the family. He and his conspirators drove my dad to suicide with false accusations."

"I read about some of this in the papers when John was killed. Wait, are you the guy that killed John Richmond?"

Harold nodded, "We managed to keep my name out of the news."

Bill took a few steps away and then turned, "The papers said a resident had stopped John from killing a doctor and a housekeeper. That was Joshua and Maria?"

Harold nodded.

"How does that tie in with Chuck?"

Harold answered, "John knew Chuck. I've always thought there was a connection there, but I've never been able to figure it out."

"What does Darla think?"

Harold answered, "She said it looks suspicious, but it probably isn't connected."

"I have a question. How did it feel when you killed John?"

CHAPTER 16

Harold turned and let his legs hang over the rock. Bill thought his eyes looked sadder and small wrinkles traced across his forehead.

Harold answered, "If I'm honest, it felt good when I killed him. John Richmond had destroyed my parents, their business and attempted to kill anyone who was still around. All my hurt and anger were directed at him in my rage. The power of going berserk, controlling it, focusing it, that was a rush, like a drug.

"Afterwards, all the guilt and regret of my actions overwhelmed me. I realized I had taken a life. Even in self-defense, I felt like a murderer because of the joy I took in my actions."

Bill walked up closer to Harold, "That's what I'm feeling."

Harold asked, "Are you having nightmares?"

"I mean, Joshua told me they are memories of our sessions together. I've seen Lori in some."

Harold asked, "Any demons or the people you killed."

"Oh, nothing like that."

Harold let out a sigh, "You're lucky. I was haunted for months. Darla, Garcia, and Joshua finally helped me understand that God had given me this gift. Without my ability, they might all be dead by now.

"Joshua explained the momentary joy of my actions was focused on protecting others, not harming them."

Bill crossed his arms, "So, you think our ability to tear people apart is a gift from God?"

Harold shrugged, "That's above my paygrade."

"What's that supposed to mean?"

Harold answered, "It means I'm not God. I didn't make me. I just have to learn to live with who I am and try to be the best person I can possibly be. That whole Christian thing I grew up with; the grace of Jesus. Either forgiveness is real, or it's not. If it's real, God is molding me into the person I was created to be. If it's not, then maybe John Richmond and his pleasure island we're standing on was right."

Bill asked, "This belonged to John?"

Harold nodded.

"So, you think God gave you this island for killing John?"

Harold stared intently at Bill for several seconds and then answered. "You really are cynical."

"I think I have a right to be."

Harold answered, "Maybe. To answer your question, the CIA gave me this island. It's a long story. I'm not fond of it, and if I can offload it someday, I will. I take it you don't believe in God."

Bill walked to the water's edge, "I used to believe. I don't know anymore. What kind of God takes away the only family an orphan finally has?"

Bill turned and looked at Harold, who was slipping off the rock. He walked over and put his arm around Bill's shoulder.

Harold answered, "I don't know. I can tell you that Bible you used to read is full of people who experienced massive loss. Later God brought them into something better to accomplish his purpose. It's funny; we always sat in church and sang hymns about these stories or talked about these people in Sunday School.

"Everyone seems to forget that these people had no idea what was going on at the time. Jonah inside the fish, I'm sure he thought he was dead. David having Saul throws spears at him during fits of rage. Elijah on the run from Jezebel. Job losing his family and everything he ever owned. We know the end of the stories, but they didn't."

The two began to walk back towards the trail.

Bill finally asked, "So, you're saying I should have faith?"

Harold answered, "Yes."

Bill mumbled, "Easier said than done."

He slipped his shoulder from Harold's embrace, and the two quietly walked back to the main house. Darla was sitting in the living room with a cocktail. The wall had been shut, and the room felt cooler and dryer.

Harold said, "I found him just where we thought."

Darla pointed at the empty loveseat. "Please, sit down and visit with us for a few minutes."

Bill sat down, and Darla picked up two drinks like her own.

Bill put up his hand, "Thank you, I'm not in the mood."

Darla smiled and put the drink in front of him. She handed Harold the other one.

She turned back to Bill and said, "Please, this will help you sleep better tonight. You've had a very hectic day. Besides, I made them myself. You wouldn't want to insult me in my own home, would you?"

Bill reached for his glass, "Well when you put it that way, I can't insult my newly found brother's wife. What sort of drink is it?"

Darla answered, "It's a mojito."

Bill smiled and gave her a nod. The rum drink's cool mint flavor refreshed his pallet, and Bill drank half the glass before putting it down. He sat back on the sofa and put his arm up on the back. Harold sat in the corner with a permanent smile partially exposed under his red beard.

Bill pointed to Harold's face, "How long do you plan on keeping that thing?"

Darla interjected, "Thank you. He won't listen to me. I want to see my husband's face, but he says he won't shave until we catch Chuck and we can get out of here."

Harold answered them both, "It's like a vow."

Bill said, "It sounds more like an excuse."

He began to laugh at his own joke, sat up, doubled over, and continued laughing. His head felt light, and the room started to swim. He stopped laughing and tried to focus.

Bill said, "Excuse me, this drink is hitting me harder than I thought. I think I better go to my bungalow."

Darla leaned forward, "Please, don't try. You may fall down before you get there."

"Did you slip me mickey?"

Darla answered, "Yes."

Harold asked, "You drugged my brother's drink?"

Darla put up her hands, "Please, it isn't like that. It's just a little drug to help him relax and remember."

Bill's slurred, "Truth serum."

"Exactly."

"Why?" asked Harold.

Darla answered, "We have your brother's phone records. We know Chuck called him at his condo when he lived in uptown Charlotte. However, your brother doesn't remember anything about that conversation. According to what I've read, Chuck called him multiple times in a span of just a few minutes.

"For months, we've thought Chuck was after Garcia. I can't deny your brother's observation that Chuck wants you. I want to know why. Chuck may have said something to Bill in that phone call that will help us figure out what he's really after and why."

Harold's voice began to sound distant to Bill, "But this is our house. He's my brother. We agreed to keep your CIA work and our family separate."

Darla answered, "My work is our family right now. I'm sorry, dear, but Bill needs to relax and feel comfortable for this drug to work. He's with the brother who has tracked him for years and loves him more than himself. I love you, so I can't help but look at Bill as family."

Bill slurred, "Am I okay?"

Darla's voice penetrated through his foggy mind. "Yes. The drug only helps you relax. We use this on people who try to hide the truth. I know you want to tell me the truth, but your brain has blocked the memory. We are going to try to help you remember."

Bill said, "Like Joshua."

Darla slid forward on the sofa. The sound resounded in Bill's ears, and he winced.

Darla spoke softly, "Sorry, the sounds will calm down in a few minutes. Can you focus on me?"

Bill nodded.

Darla continued, "Good. Do you remember your condo at the Vue in uptown Charlotte?"

Bill whispered, "Yes."

Darla asked, "Can you tell me what it looked like?"

Bill's lips curved up slightly. "It was beautiful. I could look out at the skyscrapers every morning. The sun would reflect off the glass and steel. At night they glowed from the bankers' offices working late into the night. The windows would cast an auburn light from the building's silhouettes."

Darla interrupted. "Yes, it sounds beautiful. What was it like inside? Could people see inside any of your rooms?"

Darla's voice sounded normal, and Bill eased back into the loveseat. The sound of sliding fabric no longer echoed in his head. His body felt heavy, relaxed. "My condo had an open floorplan. Depending on what building you were working in, you could see inside it if I left my blinds open."

Darla asked, "Do you remember a night around eleven pm when you received a phone call?"

Bill's eyes narrowed and then widened, "Yes."

Darla leaned in, "Do you remember what you were doing that night?"

Bill nodded. "Lori was with me. We had gone to dinner."

"Did Lori live with you?"

Bill answered, "Sometimes."

Darla's eyes seemed to drill into Bill, and he stared directly back into her eyes. Their dark circles felt warm, inviting. She continued, "What were you doing that night?"

A large smile spread across Bill's face, "Seducing each other."

Darla's stare didn't waver. "What happened when the phone rang?"

Bill frowned, and his brow furrowed, "Chuck interrupted my evening."

Darla continued, "What did Chuck ask you?"

Bill answered, "He asked me if I knew Harold. I told him he had the wrong number. He called back, and I told him again. I tossed the phone onto the table, and it hit the floor. He never called back."

Darla continued, "Focus, did he mention anyone else, or anything else?"

Bill continued looking at Darla. "Oh, he mentioned Joshua. He said maybe Joshua had hidden Harold from me for some reason." Bill looked over at Harold, "He was right."

Harold patted Bill's shoulder, "It's alright."

Bill looked back at Darla, and she said, "You've done great."

She finally broke her gaze and then left the room. Bill sat back and focused on keeping his eyes open, but he lost the battle. Darla returned to the room with some orange juice and handed it to Bill.

Darla said, "Drink this. It has some added vitamins. You'll feel better when you wake up."

Bill had to use both hands to get the glass to his mouth, and he finished off the orange juice before lowering his glass. He leaned forward to set it on the table, but his body continued its momentum. Harold caught him.

Harold said, "Why don't you stay in the guest room tonight."

"Is it close?" mumbled Bill.

"Much closer."

Bill nodded.

Harold stooped and put Bill's arm over his shoulder. The two clumsily made their way into a part of the house Bill hadn't seen. Harold turned on the light. A queen-sized bed with a nightstand and chair filled most of the room. Harold leaned Bill against the side of the bed.

He pointed towards a door that was opened to a dark room. "That's your bathroom. You can shower in there in the morning. We'll get you some clean clothes."

Bill nodded once and fell onto the bed. He could feel Harold taking off his shoes, and then the world went black.

CHAPTER 17

"Wake up, bro."

Bill slowly opened his eyes. A red fuzzy blob floated in the air, and he blinked a few times. Harold's bearded face hovered over him.

Harold said, "Hurry up, you need to get going."

Bill grabbed the back of this head as he sat up.

Harold pointed at the nightstand, "Darla said you might have a small headache. There's a coffee and multi-vitamin right here. Joshua brought over some clothes; they're in the bathroom."

Bill asked, "How late is it?"

Harold answered, "It's eight in the morning."

Bill grabbed his coffee and took a sip of the steaming liquid.

Harold said, "You need to get moving. You can drink that after you dress."

Bill scowled, "What's the hurry?"

"Garcia's coming. He wants the crew together when he arrives. Darla said he'll be here in under twenty-minutes."

Bill stretched his back and massaged the back of his neck. "I'll do my best."

Harold said, "No, you have to be at the meeting. I've learned that the CIA is very serious about these things. I'll see you out on the patio in fifteen minutes."

Bill protested, "You said we had twenty minutes."

"It's CIA time."

Harold left, and Bill waved off the closing door as he made his way to the bathroom. True to Harold's word, a pair of Bermuda shorts and a tan linen shirt sat folded on the counter along with Bill's undergarments. He took a quick shower and walked out of his room in ten minutes with the coffee in his hand.

Everyone was seated and conversing among themselves. Coffee mugs lined the table except for one seat across from Harold. Harold's chair from the night before sat empty with a cup of steaming black coffee in front of it. The crew grew quiet as Bill sat down.

Bill looked around, "Please, don't let me interrupt."

Darla asked, "How are you feeling?"

Bill answered, "The headache is getting better. Why didn't you just ask Joshua to help you instead of slipping me a mickey?"

Joshua interjected, "I wasn't consulted."

Darla looked between Joshua and Bill. "Since I didn't know what sort of information might be locked in Bill's head, I had to keep the number of people involved to a minimum."

"So, spouses have clearance?"

Harold answered, "My company makes nukes for the government. You can't do that without a high-security clearance."

Bill leaned forward towards Harold, "Is that why we had our little chat on the beach? You're were trying to win my loyalty for Darla?"

Harold scowled and shook his head. "No. We're family."

Bill sat back, "Yea, so you've said a few dozen times. Maybe we are, and maybe we aren't. I just lost my family, I'm not in a hurry to replace them."

The group sat silent and drank their coffee. Frank walked over and topped off Bill's mug when Garcia's voice emanated from inside the house, causing Darla to rise, and everyone followed suit.

Garcia was dressed in tan khaki shorts, A flowered button-down shirt, socks, tennis shoes, a straw hat, and sunglasses. He said, "Everyone, please have a seat."

Bill sat and watched Garcia wander to the front of the table. Garcia took the empty seat next to him and grabbed Bill's hand. Frank put the decanter on the table and left.

Garcia said, "Darla told me your meeting at the airport took an unexpected turn. I'm so glad you're alright." He released Bill's hand.

His sunglasses scanned the table. When he got to Maria, she pointed to her nose's bridge. Garcia removed his sunglasses and continued studying the remainder of the group. It reminded Bill of Dr. Adam when he acted as softball coach at the orphanage.

Garcia's gaze moved past the group into the empty house. "I wanted to get you guys together and give you a heads up. Alice is on her way here."

Darla rested her forehead against the palms of her hands. Harold let out a low whistle.

Bill asked, "Who's Alice?"

Darla answered, "Our boss."

"She's everyone's boss?"

Garcia answered, "No, just Darla and me."

"So, she's what. CIA, DHS, some other acronym?" asked Bill.

"Something like that," replied Garcia. "Look, Alice confirmed Carol is in the hands of a human trafficking organization, and if Chuck hands her over, we'll never find her."

Bill slammed his hand on the table, "No!"

Garcia grabbed his hand, "Calm down. We have a plan. Alice has a plan, and she's joining us in our rescue of Carol."

Bill clenched his fist under Garcia's hand, "I better be involved."

Garcia patted his hand, "Relax, you're at this table for a reason.

Darla asked, "When will Alice arrive?"

A familiar woman's voice caught Bill's attention. Bill stood before anyone in the group could move. "Cindy, why are you here?"

Garcia stood up, and the remainder of the group followed suit. Bill recognized her black hair pulled back in a ponytail and her fit figure. Garcia said, "This is Alice."

Alice held up her hand, "Relax, Mr. Johnson and I met at the hospital. As I mentioned at the time, the less you knew, the better. I apologize for my false name."

Bill asked, "So, you're FBI?"

"Also, for lying about my department. I'm with the CIA."

Bill's eyes danced for a moment, and he said, "Is anything that's happened true?"

Alice smiled and said, "Please, have a seat. We need to discuss getting your friend back and Chuck."

Bill nodded, and everyone sat down. Frank appeared with a mug of coffee, and Alice leaned up against a column rather than sit down.

She began, "First, let me commend Bill for the way he has handled himself. I know agents who had to take a sabbatical after their first week, and it wasn't nearly as dramatic as yours. Regarding your friend with the smashed skull in Wilkesboro, I'm happy to say he was just a mercenary. In fact, everyone at the hanger was a hired gun.

"This is excellent news for us. It means Chuck no longer has a team of people he can trust. I imagine Nigel was his last connection before Bill took him out. Of course, this also means Chuck is more unpredictable.

"I believe it's safe to say the CIA is no longer on his target list. He seems obsessed with Harold. We don't believe he's planning on killing Harold. It could be leverage to get the CIA to back off. It could be more sinister and involve Harold's company and nuclear weapons. We aren't sure at this point."

Bill interrupted, "Maybe someone else wants Harold."

Alice pushed herself off the pillar, against the back of Harold's chair, and stared down into Bill's eyes. "Mr. Johnson, that's an interesting thought. What makes you say that?"

Bill cleared his throat, "Well, I'm not an agent, but it seems like Chuck would have gone into hiding and waited for things to calm down. I deal with people's money every day. There are a thousand places around the world that launder money and keep gray money safe. I imagine Chuck has plenty of resources to keep himself comfortable and out of sight for decades.

"Also, why come after me at all? Harold and I didn't know each other."

Joshua interrupted, "Your brother's one goal in his life was to find you. Chuck knew about that somehow."

Bill continued, "But why put himself at risk for Harold if this is about revenge or leverage? He has way too many people looking for him now. Either this Chuck is an idiot, or someone is pulling his strings."

Alice took a step back and took a long sip of coffee. Her lips smiled as she lowered her mug. She looked across the table at Joshua, "I thought you told us Harold had the higher I.Q?"

Harold spoke up, "Doc, you said that?"

Joshua raised his hands up, "Please, don't place any weight on those tests. It's just how you boys tested at the time. It doesn't mean anything now."

Alice turned back to Bill, "You have a very analytical mind."

Bill answered, "You can't succeed in the stock market if you don't."

Alice walked toward Garcia's position and took his chair. Frank appeared from the house's shadows with a wicker chair and sat it next to Harold. Garcia took a seat.

Alice said, "I'm interested in your opinion of our plan to rescue your friend.

"I sent word through channels to Chuck that we will meet him at Crossroads Key. We all know the terrain, and I'm assuming Chuck has not been back there. I have a well-hidden bunker, and there is only one side of the island accessible by boat.

"I'll be in the bunker until Chuck makes landfall with Carol. Then I'll make my way through the grasses and get a scope on Mr. McGill. There's lots of open water, so it will be easy enough to position a couple of satellites to scan the area for any backup on Chuck's side. My plan is to have Harold and Bill both wait for Chuck."

Garcia asked, "Chuck's okay with Harold and Bill being at the meeting?"

Alice replied, "He won't know, but it's not a problem. Chuck can be unpredictable, but he can't argue with Bill's desire to take Carol home. Chuck will likely assume we wouldn't put Bill in harm's way after our last encounters."

Bill leaned towards Alice, "What encounters?"

Bill couldn't help noticing Garcia and Alice glance at Harold. He looked over at Harold and asked, "What encounters?"

Harold answered, "It's not important right now. I can tell you later."

Bill asked, "Who died?"

Harold replied, "Only some horrible people."

Maria spoke up, "They shot Darla."

Alice glared towards Maria, and Maria returned the favor. Garcia and Joshua looked nervous.

Darla cleared her throat. "If we can get back to the plan. Am I to assume we'll grab Chuck as soon as Carol is safe with Bill?"

Alice nodded and continued to glare at Maria.

Bill looked over at Harold. "What's to stop me from killing the man responsible for my family's death? Would you try to stop me?"

Alice's cool touch got Bill's attention. She looked into his eyes with compassion and softly warned, "Please, don't make me shoot you."

Bill pulled back his hand and said, "Whatever. I may be in the mood to be shot."

Alice replied, "Mr. Johnson, Chuck is not a stupid man. He seems to understand your brother's berserk tendencies, and I have no doubt he knows what you did to Nigel. He will be armed, but Chuck likely wouldn't shoot you. He would shoot Carol as soon as you took a step towards him. Whether you collapse in grief or you tear him apart, Chuck would consider it a personal victory over you."

Bill responded, "Whatever. I don't know anything about this key, but your plan sounds alright. I don't care if you shoot me or not. If Chuck gets squirrely, I'm taking him out."

Alice replied, "Then we'll make sure Mr. McGill is convinced the exchange is legitimate."

CHAPTER 18

Bill stood on the sunbathing pads with Harold near the covered hot tub. He hung on to the glass wall that pressed against his thigh. The top deck gently swayed in the relatively calm waters. Harold breathed deeply and looked up at the sky. The large yacht gently slid along the calm Gulf waters. Off to the left sat Cayo Agua. A few sunbathers who had arrived in their small craft sat sunbathing while others swam in its shallows.

The yacht gently maneuvered between the small desert keys that dotted the sea. The tepid air caressed Bill's face, and a smile formed on his lips. He closed his eyes and took in the sea air through his nostrils. There was something about being aboard the ship that was different than the island. It was quieter. The wind carried the diminishing sunbathers' laughter, and Bill felt his body relax.

He released the glass railing and let his legs adjust to the rolling at the top of the ship. Harold elbowed him and pointed. A small pod of dolphins swam on the yacht's starboard side just ahead of the bow. One jumped into the air and flipped.

He spoke reverently to Harold, "I'm beginning to understand why you have this boat."

Harold took in a deep breath and let it out. The grin never left his furry face. He said, "She's a ship. I would have never thought of buying myself something like this, but it came along with the island. Well, I sort of asked for her."

Bill's eyebrow went up, "Sort of?"

Harold answered, "Yea. The ship originally belonged to John Richmond. I'm still amazed the man actually owned something fun and inviting. Anyway, I decided if I had to work with the CIA, I should get something for my trouble. When the opportunity presented itself, I asked for the yacht."

"John named the ship Sweet Salvation?"

Joshua's voice behind Bill made him jump. "No, Richard called it Sweet Revenge. Your brother was not fond of that name."

Harold spoke up, "She's been a refuge for us when we had to deal with Chuck. Also, I feel closer to God when I'm out here."

Bill scowled, "So, like a Joel Olsteen thing."

Harold replied, "Nothing like that. I feel this way on the cabin cruiser when I go out fishing. I like the yacht because my friends and family can experience this with me."

Joshua said to Bill, "Maybe this will allow you to reflect. I understand we have some time before we get to Crossroad Key."

Bill asked, "How far is it?"

Harold answered, "Not as far as you'd think. Darla and Garcia want to make sure the ship can't be tracked. So, we take a few days and meander around the ocean. Satellites are tracking the ship and any craft around us. The underwater microphones that the U.S. put on the seafloor during the cold war listen for underwater craft."

Bill said, "That must keep them busy. We're in the Caribbean; boats are coming and going constantly."

Harold only nodded.

Joshua spoke up, "I almost forgot, Darla said after you're done introducing your brother to your beloved up here, she wants you all down on the main deck. We're meeting at the aft dining table to discuss our plans."

Bill asked, "Again?"

Joshua nodded, "It's training. When your brain doesn't need to think about your actions, you'll make the right decisions even in the worst of circumstances."

Harold rolled his eyes, "Because these meetings with Chuck always go according to plan. Well, let's go."

The three men headed down the spiral staircase and then down a second set of stairs to the main deck. Maria, Darla, Garcia, and Alice all sat waiting. Harold pointed Bill to the seat next to him. Joshua joined Maria.

Joshua spoke up first, "I still don't like my wife being here."

Alice responded. "Your lovely wife educated me on the way she has been left behind on every operation. There's no reason she can't stay on board ship while we are on the island. She'll be in no danger."

Joshua responded, "What about when we are transporting Chuck?"

"We'll have ships in the area. Of course, that's assuming we take Chuck alive."

Garcia said, "Hang on, I thought this whole operation was to bring Chuck in."

Alice responded, "It is. However, things happen in the field, especially at that location. I'm not going to risk any of you. If Chuck gets too unpredictable for my liking, I'm going to put a bullet in his head."

Bill said, "Then why not let me kill him?"

Joshua asked, "You don't have any regrets about killing those other men?"

Bill was silent.

Darla spoke up, "Let us handle the violence. This isn't something you signed up for. Your job is to get Carol out of harm's way. Now, tell me exactly what you're supposed to do."

Bill started to mindlessly drum his fingers. "I wait next to Harold. Chuck will likely be armed, so I shouldn't move until I'm told, or he'll kill Carol. Carol and I will meet halfway between Chuck and Harold, and I take Carol back beyond Harold towards a foxhole that's out of sight."

Alice said, "Perfect. Harold, what do you do?"

"I walk to Chuck and pretend to go willingly. The first chance I get, I go for the gun because Chuck likely won't shoot me. After I remove the gun, you, Garcia, and Darla will swoop in to save the day."

Darla said, "Darling, don't sound so cynical. Alice will be spotting through her sniper scope. We will have no problem coming sooner if there's a need."

Bill asked, "What if Harold can't get the gun?"

Harold smiled, "I force the situation."

Bill asked, "How?"

"Darla's been training me. I've learned all my rage does me little good if I don't do a better job at directing it."

Bill answered, "But, when I went berserk, I was able to shoot like a marksman, and I haven't had any training."

Joshua answered, "We still don't know what causes this condition and why it only shows up in some people regularly. The rush of adrenaline, the hypersensitivity, and honestly, perhaps some divine intervention worked in your favor.

"I've watched over Harold during his training with Darla. Proper defense training is as much about self-control as it is attacking. Harold can focus his energy better."

Harold spoke up, "It's helped me not only fight better but work better. I'm always evaluating how I'm spending my time, and if the solutions and ideas I come up with for PDS are worth pursuing."

Alice said, "Alright, let's get back on point. Once Chuck is taken into custody, he will be brought to the yacht."

Harold interrupted, "I still don't see why it has to be my ship."

Alice looked him in the eye and continued, "He's being brought to the yacht because we have some questions that need to be answered in open waters. We've designed a cell, excuse me, stateroom below that will be able to hold him.

"The doctor will then assist us in our interrogation. Once we have the answers we want, we're off to Guantanamo Bay to drop Chuck off at his new residence."

Maria spoke up, "I don't like you using my husband's talents for torture."

Joshua protested, "It's not torturing. I'm going to work with Darla. The CIA's drugs won't work on a man like Chuck, but their drugs and my understanding of hypnosis may be enough to get us the information we want."

Maria asked, "What if he refuses to talk?"

Alice gave Maria an icy stare, "He'll talk."

Maria glared back at Alice, "Torture."

Alice answered, "Chuck has killed thousands in his lifetime and helped groups like ISIS get access to explosives and drones. Tell me, whose life should I save, Chuck or a ten-year-old child who is being sex trafficked to perverts in an ISIS offshoot?"

Maria waved her off, "I've seen this growing up. One day you're torturing a cartel member, and a week later, it's a political rival."

Alice answered, "That's not who we are."

"We'll see."

Garcia chimed in, "Are we all set then?"

Alice looked over at Garcia. Garcia murmured, "Sorry, I'm used to running the team."

Alice looked around the table. "I know things are tense. They always are before an operation. Bill, take some time to get to know Harold and Garcia a little better. These meetings sometimes go awry, and the more we trust one another, the more likely we'll all come out alive the other side."

Bill nodded.

Garcia turned to Alice, "May I?"

Alice nodded.

Garcia said, "Meeting adjourned."

CHAPTER 19

Hot water ebbed and flowed against Bill's chest. When the hot water receded, his skin felt sticky in the humid air. The low-hanging sun was still hot, and his once pale skin looked darker and redder. Bill reached for his cocktail. The chilly fruit juices with a splash of rum felt cool against his throat.

Harold sat across from him in the round hot tub. His eyes were closed, and his head tilted up towards the heavens. Harold's face and head were mostly a mass of red hair, protecting him from the slowly sinking sun. The yacht gently rocked in the water and had appeared to put his brother to sleep.

The sound of footsteps coming up the ladder made Harold raise his head. Garcia appeared in a teal and yellow bathing suit with surfers printed on it. He had on his sunglasses and held what appeared to be two rum runners in large glasses.

"Mind if I join you, boys?"

Harold waved him over and put his head back against the railing. Garcia eased into the water. He put one drink on the decking near him and swallowed down half a glass of the other before setting it down.

Garcia said, "Frank sure knows how to make a good rum runner."

Harold spoke without raising his head, "What brings you up here? You don't wear those sunglasses without reason."

Garcia responded, "The sun's bright."

Harold lifted his head, "It's almost sundown. Please don't tell me you're interrupting a little quiet brother time for no reason."

"I didn't realize I'm intruding."

Bill said, "You're not."

Harold caught Bill's attention by raising his index finger from the rail where it rested. "You may be sorry. The last time Garcia and I had a quiet chat, I couldn't drink coffee for a month."

Garcia said, "That's not true."

A grin poked out from Harold's hairy face.

Bill said, "I take it that's an inside joke."

Both men nodded.

Bill asked, "What's the deal between Maria and Alice?"

Harold answered, "Oh, you don't cross paths with Maria. I grew up with her. She was like the older sister most guys loved and feared. She would cover my tracks when it would keep me out of trouble with my parents, but if my friends and I did anything she didn't approve of, she would either go to Mom and Dad or face off with my buddies."

Bill asked, "Did Alice do something to you?"

Garcia interjected, "Not to Harold. Joshua and Maria were at the orphanage studying your case, and Maria hit it off with the orphans. We had to pull them out of the area when our sting with Chuck went sideways. That woman does not like to be kept at home or anywhere she doesn't have work to do."

Harold interjected, "Don't forget Haidar shooting Darla. Thankfully, it was a flesh wound in the shoulder. Unfortunately, once Maria considers you family, she takes any sort of attack very personally, even when it doesn't involve her."

Bill asked, "So, she blames Alice?"

Harold answered, "Not without cause. Joshua has been involved with most of our work before and after the orphanage. That only made Maria angrier. She feels like a third wheel, or at least unappreciated. Alice made the mistake of talking with her. Let's just say Maria found their first conversation a little condescending."

Garcia asked Harold, "What's the temperature to-day in the tub?"

Harold answered, "I have it down to one hundred, so we can stay in here as long as we like."

Garcia answered, "Good. I wanted to talk to Bill, but you're welcome to stay. It's about Chuck, Joshua, and yourself. You already know the story."

Harold laid his head back on the rail, "I like a good bedtime story."

Garcia turned his sunglasses to Bill. "I know you're wondering how you ended up here. I can provide you some of the answers if you want them."

Bill leaned forward, "Are you kidding?"

Garcia said, "I've known about you and your brother since Harold was adopted as a toddler. I was a friend of Richard Brown, his father. Well, it was an assignment, but we became friends. I had asked for a job stateside. The CIA basically gave me babysitting duty over Richard and Barbara, Harold's mom. We were still in the cold war, and anyone dealing with nuclear weapons was a high-security risk.

"Richard and I hit it off, and he confided in me that he was planning to adopt a son since they couldn't have kids. I told him I might have a lead for him in North Carolina. Before he was at the orphanage, Joshua worked in Army Intelligence. He mostly profiled various terrorists and Soviet spies. He hated the work, but it gave him some practical experience while deciding what he wanted to do with his life and education.

"So, Harold was adopted by the Browns. After they brought him home, Harold begged them to adopt you. However, there was a problem. Harold's biological father."

Harold interrupted, "Sperm donor and rapist."

Bill said, "What?"

Harold raised his head and looked at Bill. "My uncle raped our mother, and I was the result."

Garcia jumped in, "It's true. To make matters worse, he had tried to get custody, but the courts obviously said no. Harold's biological father got nabbed a short time later for smuggling drugs. He jumped bail and has been missing ever since.

"We hid Harold's adoption from his biological father by changing his given name. California seals the adoption records, so we knew Harold would not be traceable. However, we were afraid that if the Browns adopted you, you would lead Harold's father right to the Browns. For security reasons, I couldn't let that happen."

Bill asked, "Why couldn't you just change my name?"

Garcia answered, "Your mother, Rachael, wouldn't give up custody. Although she initially hated Harold because of the rape, therapy and time had softened her heart. She didn't want to lose another child. If Richard, Harold's father, had fought Rachael in court, the adoption would have gone through a drawn-out legal drama. Given Richard's stature in the community out west, it would have made the news, at least locally. That could have attracted the attention of Harold's, um, sperm donor at some point. I worked with Adam and Joshua to make sure the two of you were separated."

Bill asked, "So that's why Joshua thought Harold and I might be dangerous if we were brought together?"

Garcia answered, "Somewhat. He was also concerned with Harold's outrage and your previous episodes before he hypnotized you. In any case, I couldn't allow the adoption to keep Richard safe.

"This past year has been one misstep after another. I feel like we've all been one step behind Chuck. He was involved with the men who blackmailed Harold's dad with fake evidence of an affair. After Richard killed himself, Chuck backed away. John Richmond decided he would try and take Parabolic Defense Systems himself, and the rest is history."

Harold nodded.

Bill rubbed his forehead, "What does that have to do with Chuck, and me? I think we still have some pieces missing. Chuck should be under a rock living the retired life, thanking God, he made it out alive."

Garcia continued, "When we first engaged Chuck, he was interested in buying weapons on the black market from Harold. We had led Chuck to believe that PDS was about to go bankrupt and Harold was desperate. On the day of the sting, things turned ugly. Chuck detected a faulty computer chip and discovered our trackers. All hell broke loose. The only reason we survived was Darla and Harold. They had previously saved Chuck's life from an employee who tried to kill him.

"Chuck got away. He led us to believe he wanted revenge, to prove to people he was still in charge. This entire time we thought he was targeting me and possibly Alice if he found out about her. Now, we don't know what he wants, and we don't know why."

Bill asked, "Could any of this link to Harold's father?"

Harold interrupted, "Sperm rapist."

Garcia answered, "Possibly. I just don't know why he would be doing this now?"

Bill asked, "Do you know his name?"

"Yes."

"What is it?" asked Bill.

Harold mumbled, "Monster."

Garcia answered, "That's need to know."

Bill asked, "Does Harold know it?"

Harold jumped in, "No. It's probably just as well. I might kill him if I met him."

Garcia continued, "I just wanted you to understand a little bit of what's going on. Harold has wanted to be with you since you were kids. I know you've lost the family you were hoping to have, but you do have a brother who loves you. No matter what happens with Chuck, Harold is still your brother."

Bill sighed. Garcia finished off the other half of his first glass and started on the second.

Bill finally answered. "I appreciate that. I just want you to know, my anger with Chuck isn't about all of this. It's about Lori. Chuck took away not only my wife to be but my child. No offense to my brother, but he can't replace them."

"None taken," said Harold.

Garcia took off his sunglasses, placed them next to his empty glass, and looked Bill in the eye. "I can appreciate what you're feeling. I'm protective of the people I love too, but you need to remember this whole thing is greater than you. Chuck is the only person who knows why he wants your brother. It could relate to anything. Nukes, conventional weapons, maybe it's even someone seeking revenge for what happened with John Richmond. We don't know.

"If you kill Chuck, we may not find out, and your brother and his family could still be in danger."

Bill slid his hands under the water and stared at his palms. He finally looked up, "I'll do my best, but if he tries to hurt Carol, all bets are off."

Garcia slid his sunglasses back on. "Fair enough. I'll see you at dinner, gentlemen."

Garcia pushed himself out of the hot tub, threw a dry towel over his shoulder, grabbed his two glasses, and went dripping down the staircase.

CHAPTER 20

The sea spray burned Bill's eyes, and the Kodiak bumped against his butt mercilessly. He looked back over his shoulder and saw Harold smiling at the controls of the outboard motor.

Bill hollered over the roar of the engine, "Do you have to hit the top of every wave?"

Harold hollered back, "Sorry, it's a little bumpy."

Bill turned and faced the front. The image of the yacht had long since disappeared. Harold had sworn the island would appear soon, but Bill was beginning to think Harold might have an issue with his sense of direction. The cold, wet wind permeated his jacket and skin.

Bill closed his eyes for a moment and spoke quietly under the engine's cacophony and the Kodiak slapping against the waves.

"Maybe you are there. I don't know. Please, don't let anything happen to Carol. She is the only person left who understands me. You've taken everything else from me. Please don't take her."

Harold hollered, "There it is."

Bill looked up. A small dot on the horizon began to take shape. The few palm trees on the key started to emerge, and then the rest of the island started coming into view. There were at least three boats on the beach. Harold slowed their craft slightly until the unmistakable figure of Darla emerged from a small hill. Harold opened the accelerator, and Bill nearly fell over backward.

The engine cut off a few feet from the beach, and Bill leaned back before Harold said a word. They slid up on to the sand and made an abrupt stop. Garcia walked up wearing his usual tan and white with a wide brim straw hat and sunglasses as the men were getting out of the boat.

Garcia said, "Nice stop." He pointed several yards to their right. "I want you both to go over there and check out the foxholes I've made. If there is any shooting, I want you both inside them. Bill, if Carol is with you, toss her in and jump on top of her."

Bill and Harold walked over to find two deep holes dug in the sand with a slight bump around them. Bill looked around. The handful of workers appeared to be navy. Everyone was spending more time disappearing over the small hill and coming back than worrying about the beach where the meeting was to take place.

Harold said, "Hang here for a minute. I'm heading over to check in with Darla."

Harold headed up the hill, and Bill crossed his arms. The seconds started to tick by, and Bill didn't feel like spending his time focusing on what was about to happen. He wandered to the top of the hill when Alice's voice came from the foliage on his left.

"Mr. Johnson, I wasn't aware you were needed up here."

Bill turned to see Alice emerge from the brush with an earplug hanging by a small threaded wire draped around her neck.

Bill said, "Sorry, I'm just trying to figure out what's going on."

Alice pulled him over off the narrow path. "That's alright. I have a couple of minutes before I need to suit up."

Bill asked, "Why is the military here?"

Alice answered, "International waters and they have the equipment we need. We can't have people nearby, that's why this key was chosen. So, we have ears and eyes hidden around the island. Help is still thirty minutes away, but every second counts. If they hear trouble, these people will come in locked and loaded."

"I still think we should take him out as soon as Carol is safe."

Alice gave him an icy stare. "We have an agreement."

Bill waved her off, "Yea, I haven't forgotten. Don't forget, though, if Chuck makes one move to hurt Carol, our agreement ends."

Alice answered, "Look around you. I have the situation well in hand."

"We'll see."

Alice turned on her heel and looked over her shoulder, "Time to get back to work."

In a few steps, she disappeared, and Bill took that as his cue to return to the beach. He had barely gotten his feet on the sand when the sound of multiple footsteps came from behind. He hurried out of the way. Several young men and women carried various boxes to the boats and sped out of sight in minutes.

Harold came strolling over the hill and hollered down, "Good, you're still here. I thought you might wander off. Darla said Chuck's been spotted by our drone. We won't have to wait too much longer."

Bill and Harold stood in silence. Both men scanned the sea. The only thing that rose from the horizon was an occasional bird. Bill thought he heard a motor traveling along the sea breeze a few times, but nothing appeared.

Bill asked, "I thought you said he'd be here soon."

Harold looked down at his watch, "Yea. I thought we'd see him by now. Oh, shoot."

"What is it?"

Harold turned towards the island and cocked his head. Bill strained to try and hear what Harold was listening for. A faint hum seemed to pass over the hill, but Bill dismissed it as another mind trick. Yet, it started to grow louder.

Harold said, "Chuck likes to scan the island. If he's alone, he'll circle past us at least once."

The sound of the hum soon became a dull roar and shifted direction. Before long, a shallow gunboat appeared from the corner of the island. A lone man was seen on its deck. Harold waved, and the stranger waved back as he passed the beach and continued around the island.

"Where's Carol?" asked Bill.

Harold answered, "Probably sitting out of sight with her hands tied until he feels it's safe. Chuck's a cautious guy."

The motor faded and soon returned, but this time running with less urgency. Bill could see Carol standing next to Chuck. She appeared to have her hands tied in front of her. The boat turned to the beach and softly slid into the edge of the sand. Chuck threw an anchor out on the beach.

Harold grabbed Bill's shoulder as Carol was led to the boat's edge. Chuck hopped out into the shallow water and put his arms out. Carol slid over the rail and fell into Chuck's arms. He carried her to the dry sand and gently let her down on her feet.

Chuck hollered, "See, safe and sound."

"Are you alright?" asked Bill.

Carol responded, "If this fool doesn't unshackle me, he's gonna get the beating of his life."

Chuck pulled out a large bowie knife and held up his free hand. "Just taking off the rope. I'm afraid Ms. Lewis took offense at being bound, but it was for her safety and mine."

Chuck grabbed Carol's forearm and put his knife back in its hilt. The pair walked closer. Chuck stopped. "I thought I said you were coming alone, Harold. This doesn't bode well."

Bill said, "You have my friend."

Harold interjected, "How did you think Ms. Lewis was going to get home, swim?"

Chuck laughed, "Harold, you're always thinking ahead. I suppose that's why you're the boss, like me. Of course, I practice better hygiene, but we can discuss your shaving habits on our ride out of here. Billy, how have you been? It's been a while since we last talk."

Bill replied, "I thought I told you to call me Bill."

Chuck smiled, "So, you do remember me this time."

Bill snarled, "I remember you had my wife and child killed."

Chuck shook his head. "No, no. Like I said on our short phone call a few days ago, technically speaking, I had nothing to do with that. Nigel was supposed to go in, scare the people in the office, kidnap you and leave. No bloodshed or anything to make the news for more than a night. I suppose that's what I get for sending an accountant to do a man's job."

Bill growled, "It never would have happened if you hadn't sent him."

Chuck took out a cigar, lit it, and then pointed it in Bill's direction. "You need to watch that temper. It will get you into trouble."

Chuck stuck the stogie in his mouth and then reached behind his back and pulled out a large pistol. He waved it in front of him. "Harold probably knows this gun, growing up like he did, but let me explain it to you, Bill. This is a Desert Eagle. It can bring down anything I point it at, including you two and your friend. Now, relax."

Harold spoke up. "I have one question, why me? Why put yourself at risk just to pick me up."

Chuck answered, "We all have a job to do, and we all have our bosses. My employer wants me to bring you in."

"Why?" asked Harold.

Chuck waived his gun as he spoke, "He'll have to tell you that. I'm sworn to secrecy, the hazards of my trade. I can tell you he's swears no harm will come to you. Now, let's get this show on the road. The sooner I deliver you, the sooner I can rebuild my business."

"Oh, did I reduce your staff?" scoffed Bill.

Chuck answered, "You should learn some humility from your brother. The CIA dismantled most of my operation. You just helped me fire a subpar employee."

Harold asked, "What makes you think the CIA will leave you alone?"

Chuck took a long drag off his cigar. Carol waved the smoke back in his face. "Let's just say when my little assignment is done here, I'm looking for work, but enough chit chat. Let's make the swap. I'm tired of being in the sun."

Bill started to walk forward. Chuck pointed his pistol and asked, "What are you doing?"

"I take Carol, and then you get Harold."

Chuck started laughing, "Boy, you really are full of yourself. I'm afraid not, sonny. Your brother comes forward, and I release Carol, and they meet halfway."

Harold answered, "Alright."

He began towards Chuck. Carol started walking quickly towards Harold. She passed Harold before he was halfway across. Bill opened his arms, and she dove into them.

Bill whispered, "Did they touch you?"

Carol answered, "No. Chuck protected me."

Bill put his arm around her and slowly walked away towards the unseen foxhole.

Chuck hollered, "Freeze, nobody moves."

CHAPTER 21

Bill could hear his heart beating. He felt the grains of sand rolling under the heel of his shoes. The blue sky began to turn crimson as he watched the blood flow through his retinas until everything was red. Carol's breath was shallow, and Bill could feel her fear. He grasped her waist in his hands.

She whispered, "What are you doing."

His eyes darted towards her maroon figure. "When you land, roll until you land in the hole."

"Do what?"

Bill could see the hidden ridge of the foxhole several feet away. His legs relaxed, but his muscles tingled.

Bill said in a low growl, "1,2,3."

Carol's body felt lighter than he remembered. Carol let out a scream of surprise. The sound of a small canon exploded behind Bill, and he smiled in anticipation of the bullet. The ground rose under his right foot and he darted to his left. Sawgrass and bushes lay before him, and he sped in their direction.

Over his shoulder, he could hear Chuck yelling, "Move, Harold."

The sawgrass cut against his legs, and Bill dropped to all fours and dashed ahead. He had to maneuver and kill Chuck. Bill slowed, plunged to his belly, and crawled along the reddish hued sand and grass towards the lip of a small rise to see what Chuck was doing. For a moment, large trees and snow appeared before him. Bill closed his eyes and shook his head. The vision disappeared.

Chuck hollered in a sarcastic tone. "I can smell you, Bill. I know you're just over the rise. Come out if you don't want your brother killed."

Bill peaked over and saw Chuck sniffing the air, with the pistol pointed in Bill's direction.

Joshua's voice permeated his mind, "You're the wolf, stalk your prey."

Bill eased behind the rise's lip and darted towards the water on all fours. The world was a blur of maroon, red, and some pinks. Sawgrass and shrubs cut at his face as he made his way up the small hill from the water's edge, far from the beach where the drama was unfolding. He did not know how broad the key was, but he had to get behind Chuck.

Before Bill knew it, he was on the opposite side of the island.

Chuck's voice was barely perceptible, "I can smell you moving, boy."

Bill realized the ocean breeze was gently blowing behind him. A sound caught his attention. The red silhouette of a woman with a large rifle lying at the top of the hill stopped Bill in his tracks. He had to get past Alice and disguise his scent from Chuck. Without hesitation, he tore off his shirt and walked out of his pants; only his boxers remained.

Bill slipped into the water. Bill grunted when the water reached his waist. Large maroon fish darted this way and that in a sea of red as Bill slipped through the water just beneath its surface. The coral changed to sand, and he slowly rose. Chuck was further away, but they were almost even. He would have a tougher time smelling him, especially covered with saltwater.

The water slipped away from Bill's body as he eased onto the beach. He crouched down on all fours, waiting to spring.

Chuck still looked towards the hill and hollered, "I'm going to count to ten. If you don't come out, I'll shoot your brother."

Bill could see the top of Harold's head. Through the breeze, he could hear Harold's breath growing more intense.

Bill thought; *finally, we will kill the man who has destroyed our families.*

At the count of 10, sand exploded around Chuck. He grabbed at his eyes, and the air rumbled with the sound of a large weapon. First, on all fours, Bill sprung forward and rose to his feet. He let out a howl that filled the air. He could see Chuck turn towards him, and Harold sprint from the other direction with a roar.

The world exploded again, and the sand covered Chuck. His gun dropped from his hand, and Bill accelerated. Something hard violently collided with Bill. It hung on and rolled him over, and then his momentum sent him airborne. He landed and rolled to the water's edge. The red outline of a woman stood before him.

Darla's familiar voice was stern, "Stand down."
Bill growled.
Darla repeated her command. Bill felt no fear from her. He looked to his right to find Harold on top of Chuck, but instead of tearing his limbs apart, Harold

held Chuck's hands behind his back. His rage started to subside. Bill began to gasp for air, and the red universe began to regain its colors.

Bill looked back at Darla and gasped, "How did you do that?"

"Momentum and leverage. Brains over brawn."

Bill nodded and focused on breathing.

Alice yelled from the pathway on the hill, "Darla, Harold, finish securing our new friend. Bill, with me. Carol, it's safe to come out."

Bill stood and heard Carol exclaim, "Good lord, where are your clothes?"

Bill felt his face flush and looked down. His wet boxers clung to his dripping, sand-covered body. His head drooped as he began to make his way across the small beach. Garcia appeared from behind Alice and made his way down the path.

He warned Bill as they passed one another, "Get ready for a lecture."

Bill nodded and slowly made his way up the path.

Alice said, "Pick up the pace, Mr. Johnson, I have places to be."

Bill quickened his steps and stood before Alice far sooner than he desired.

Alice said, "Nice abs."

Bill raised his eyebrows.

"Walk with me, Mr. Johnson."

The two walked up the path a few yards and veered to the left.

Alice finally spoke, "Is there a reason you decided to go rogue on me?"

Bill's eyes narrowed. "Chuck tried to shoot me, to kill Carol. I'm not going to let him get away with that."

Alice's hand was cool as it gripped his bicep. "Bill, you were never in any real danger. Chuck would have shot you in the back if he wanted to kill you and if he wanted to die. He knew this was a trap. I'm just trying to figure out why he let himself get captured."

"Where were Darla and Garcia?" Asked Bill. "I snuck around you and didn't see anyone."

A large sniper rifle laid in the sand. Alice lifted the heavy weapon and laid it across her shoulders. "I never leave anything to chance."

The corner of Alice's lips curved up for a moment and then went flat, "Mr. Johnson, I knew where you were. Do you think I can't hear a grown man in the bushes? As for the other two, you saw what I wanted you to see."

Bill replied, "I don't understand."

"Camouflage. We had a lot of time to kill on the island before you showed up. Also, Dr. Zeev has been helpful. You're like an animal when you go into a rage. You only see one shade of the same color; I believe it's red due to the blood rushing through your vision."

Bill nodded.

Alice continued, "We simply used the cover we needed to stay hidden from your vision. Harold has the same limitation. I'm not a liberty to say why, but there is some concern that Chuck may possess a similar impairment. If you could have seen other colors, you would have seen Darla and Garcia quite easily.

"Now, I believe there is a matter of your clothes."

A distant, faint buzz high in the air interrupted Alice.

She dropped the rifle and said, "Get to cover."

Alice took off running towards the beach. Bill thought of Carol and ran a few yards behind Alice. He found Carol waiting at the top of the hill.

Bill grabbed her arm, "Hurry, this isn't over."

The two slid over into the taller grasses. Below Darla threw Chuck to the ground and stood over him. Garcia stood near the Kodiak, and Alice held her pistol towards the sky as if she were tracking something.

Alice hollered, "Two o'clock."

She began to fire. A wisp of smoke appeared in the sky, and Alice fell. A pool of blood began to form on the sand behind her head. Garcia unloaded his clip. While he still fired, a small explosion could be seen above, and then tiny fragments fell on to the beach and in the water.

Darla and Garcia ran towards Alice's fallen body. Harold watched over Chuck. He appeared frightened of either Harold or the sky. Garcia checked for a pulse and then ran to the edge of the beach and pulled out a satellite phone.

His voice was urgent. "Agent down."

Darla marched over to Chuck and grabbed him by the throat, "Where is it."

Chuck stood wide-eyed, shaking his head. Darla let loose her grip, took two steps back, and caught her breath.

She asked again, "Where's the ship that drone came from."

Chuck answered, "I don't know. That isn't mine, I swear."

Harold asked, "Loose ends?"

Darla answered, "I want you, Bill, and Carol to get back to the ship. Tell them to meet us at zone two. Can you remember that?"

Harold answered, "Zone two, got it. What about you, Garcia, and Chuck?"

Darla answered, "Help is on the way. We have this."

Harold nodded and pointed in Bill and Carol's direction, "You two come with me."

Bill and Carol got in, and Harold pushed them offshore.

Bill asked, "Are you sure we should leave them?"

"Darla knows what she's doing. Hey, can you move to the front? I need your weight to smooth the ride."

The air moved across Bill's exposed chest. He shivered and crossed his arms.

"Are you serious? I'll freeze."

Carol said, "I'll keep you warm."

The two sat with their arms around each other at the Kodiak's bow. Harold opened up the engine, and they hung on to the seat.

Harold hollered over the roar of the motor, "Are you sure you two didn't date?"

Bill looked back and yelled, "Just friends."

Harold nodded.

Bill hollered, "What's zone two?"

Harold answered, "Beats me, I guess we'll find out."

CHAPTER 22

Frank tied the Kodiak to the yacht's dive deck and assisted everyone out. Bill led Carol up the ladder to the main deck and stretched his lower back to help with the throbbing pain. It was not working. Harold quickly followed. Joshua and Maria came through the interior living quarters' glass doors to meet them.

Maria asked, "Is everybody alright?"

Harold walked past them and commented, "I need to speak to Captain Frank."

Joshua looked at Bill, "I see you were able to retrieve your friend."

Maria's eyes widened, "Where are your clothes?"

Bill said, "It's a long story."

Maria shook her head, "Boys."

Bill responded, "Maria, Joshua, this is my friend and former administrator, Carol Lewis."

Joshua stuck out his hand. "It's a pleasure to meet you. I'm Dr. Joshua Zeev, and this is my wife, Maria."

Maria walked up and grabbed Carol's other hand. "Come with me. Harold has a cabin ready for you. I'll show you where everything is, and you can freshen up and rest. Bill guessed at your clothes size, so I hope they fit."

Bill responded, "I saw the tags when I was sorting out some of the laundry one morning."

Maria stopped and looked at Bill and then back at Carol.

Carol asked, "You sorted my laundry? You were supposed to be in recovery."

"I got bored, and you were out."

Maria gently pulled on Carol's arm, "Please come with me."

The two women retreated to the interior of the yacht.

Joshua asked, "How far back are the others?"

"We were attacked by a drone. Alice was shot. I don't think she's going to make it. Garcia sent the three of us back immediately. He said to tell Frank to go to Zone 2."

Joshua nodded, "I don't know where that is, but I'm fairly certain that's a backup rendezvous point. You should probably get below and get dressed. Why don't you meet me on the top deck for something to drink, and you can get some food if you're hungry."

Bill headed towards his cabin. The hot shower helped the aching in his back. After a couple of Tylenol and a set of dry clothes, Bill felt better and headed to the upper deck. He ran into Maria in the hallway. Maria let him know that Carol had showered and was sound asleep in her cabin.

Joshua sat at the large, white dining table that sat mid-deck underneath a roof that gave shade from the sunshine. The doctor had a glass of beer and another drink for the empty chair that sat across him. Bill took his seat.

Bill asked, "Olde Meck?"

"Always. So, tell me, how are you doing?"

Bill took a long sip of his beer, he wiped the foam from his mouth with the back of his hand. "Okay, I guess."

"Did Alice getting shot upset you?"

Bill sat back, "To be honest, I didn't really know her that well." He leaned forward, "But I do feel like some of this may be my fault."

Joshua took a small sip of his beer. "Why?"

"Chuck got skittish halfway through the exchange. I was worried about Carol and went berserk. Well, I guess you'd call it that. I knew everything that was going on. It was weird. I didn't just enjoy the chaos and violence. I formulated a plan, and you were speaking to me in my head."

Joshua's eyes widened, "What did I say?"

"Everything changed around me for a moment. It was like we were hunting in the woods, you know, like in my dreams, or hypnosis or whatever. Anyway, you were telling me how to stalk my prey. So, that's what I did with Chuck. I stripped down to my boxers and used the ocean to hide my scent."

Joshua asked, "Did you know where you were?"

"Yea. The forest only appeared for a moment, but I was able to push it out of my head."

Both sat quietly, sipping their beers. Joshua stared at his glass and rolled it in his palms.

He asked, "Why did you think Chuck could smell you?"

Bill answered, "Because he said he could."

Joshua sat back hard in his chair.

Bill asked, "What is it?"

"He must be a berserker. I didn't want it to be true. Chuck is different from you and your brother. Your brother can control his condition when something triggers an episode, and it sounds like you're adapting. If it makes you feel better, you have progressed much faster than I thought was possible.

"But Chuck, he's a different story. From what Garcia has told me, he can exhibit the symptoms at will, and not all of them at once. Chuck is a sociopath with absolute control over a syndrome that allows him to kill, maim, and torture anyone at will."

Bill took a long slow breath. Then he lifted his glass and didn't put it down until all of the amber liquid had passed through his lips. Joshua finished his drink as well. Both men stared blankly in each other's direction.

Joshua asked, "So, why do you think you caused Alice's death?"

"She was giving me a short lecture on teamwork after we subdued Chuck. I had tried to kill Chuck, and Darla stopped me while Harold and Alice took care of Chuck. A drone showed up. Alice ran ahead to the beach from this hill we were on. She fired her pistol at it, and the drone shot her. After that, Garcia shot it out of the sky."

Joshua was silent and his head drooped, and he closed his eyes.

Bill said, "I'm sorry."

"I was saying a short prayer for her and my wife. The two of them maintained had some friction between them, but they were kindred spirits, and this will break her heart.

"Bill, you didn't cause her death. She shot at the drone, and it shot back. This is tragic, but unfortunately, this is a common hazard of the type of life these brave men and women live in order to protect us."

Bill said, "Maybe, but I feel like if I hadn't gone berserk, the situation would have been different."

Joshua shook his head. "I've dealt with Chuck. What you did may have helped. Chuck doesn't like things to get out of control. He has a hard time adjusting. I'm just surprised he only had one drone."

Bill answered, "I don't think it was his. He kept saying it wasn't, and he looked terrified."

Joshua asked, "What do the others think?"

"We were kicked off the island. I have no idea what's going on. Do you mind if I ask you a question not related to all of this?"

Joshua answered, "Of course."

"What am I supposed to do now?"

"What do you mean?"

Bill said, "My whole life, I thought I was this other person. I don't know if you could say I was good, but I was good enough. I worked hard; I was starting a family. I didn't want to hurt anyone. When it came to my employees, I treated them decently, and I never invested in any shady businesses.

"Now I've killed five people, and if I'm honest, I enjoyed it at the time. I feel like I've got this monster inside of me that might jump out at any moment. What if I get road rage one day? Will I end up chasing the guy down and ripping his arms off or killing my own wife or kid?"

Joshua asked, "Let me ask you a question. How's your faith?"

Bill rolled his eyes, "Oh, please don't tell me to read my Bible and pray. This is real life."

"So, you've given up on your faith?"

Bill answered, "I'm not sure now. I mean, I guess it's nominal. I can see where God might be answering some of my needs, like showing me a brother I didn't know I had. On the other hand, If he really is there and cared, he could have left Lori and still given me Harold. I guess I'm not seeing a connection between stories several thousand years old that happened halfway around the world and modern-day."

Joshua said, "Alright. Let me put it to you this way. I believe we are still created for one or more reasons while we are on the earth. That includes all of our strengths and faults. Take Garcia and Alice. They both put their lives on the line and also take lives. Our government has taught them how to kill without hesitation. Why do you think they only kill certain people since they can do it at any time?"

Bill shrugged, "I guess their training."

Joshua answered, "Wrong. Our government doesn't teach values like the old days. Instead, they are threatened with prison for breaking the law, but they aren't taught right and wrong. Garcia, Alice, Darla, and most of the other agents come into the CIA with a robust moral compass already in place. They understand there are absolute rights and wrongs, and they don't cross that line.

"You're the same way. Dr. Adam and I spoke regularly about you when you were growing up. Even though I left, I never really left you. We both tried to install ethical and moral truths inside you and all the children.

"Let me ask you a question. If a Mexican drug cartel offered you several million dollars to launder money for them through various trades to offshore companies, would you do it?"

Bill answered, "Of course not. Those organizations deal in death and slavery. I wouldn't want their blood money."

Joshua said, "There you go."

Joshua grabbed both glasses and headed for the bar on the nearby wall. He dropped the glasses in a container and came back with two mroe bottles of beer and popped the caps off them.

He said, "I hope you don't mind. I'm quite thirsty."

Bill answered, "Me too."

They sat and sipped on their beers until they were half empty. Bill covered his mouth and tried to fight the belch that had built up, but to no avail."

"Excuse me."

Joshua smiled and let out a long, loud burp. "No problem."

Both men laughed and took another swig.

Bill put his beer down. "So, you're saying you don't think I'll become a murdering lunatic because I know right and wrong."

Joshua nodded, "That sums it up very well."

Bill was about to ask another question when the sound of a motor in the distance caught their attention. He could see a military styled ship speeding their direction from the upper deck. The sound of heavy footsteps rattled the stairs, and Harold appeared.

He said, "Both of you, we have company coming abord. Doc, you and Maria need to stay in your cabin until the coast is clear. Bill, you're with me."

Joshua responded, "So, we're doing this?"

Harold nodded his head. Joshua pushed past Harold on the steps, and Bill stood there looking at Harold.

"Come on, bro." said Harold, "Chuck will be here in a couple of minutes."

CHAPTER 23

Bill followed Harold down the stairs while the ship gently rolled. The yacht began to make a slow turn to port. The teal waters dropped away, and the naval ship that had been racing in their direction now held a steady distance. The waters rose and fell gently at higher levels, and the breeze felt cool.

Harold stopped at the main deck. They found Frank preparing the dive deck for the craft's arrival. Bill noticed a pistol stuck into the waistband in the small of his back.

"So, this is zone 2?"

Harold answered, "Welcome to the Atlantic. I'm sorry we didn't have time to talk earlier. Captain Frank and I were busy getting things ready for Chuck's arrival. Originally, he was supposed to come with us on the Kodiak. Once the Navy got involved, we went with their backup plan to move this to deeper waters."

"I don't understand. They have Chuck. Why didn't the Navy take him to Cuba? It's their base, after all."

Frank stopped his work and turned to Bill. "This is still a CIA operation. Garcia has questions that he would like to ask without the prying eyes of the DOD."

Bill's eyes widened, "So, Maria was right about torture?"

Harold answered, "Don't worry, bro. I wouldn't let that happen on my ship. Personally, I'm not sure this scheme will work. I know Chuck, and he's a pretty strong-willed guy."

Bill walked over and sat on a nearby barstool. He propped his arm on the bar and began to drum his fingers for several seconds, and watched Frank get back to work.

"Do you know what the CIA wants? I mean, why go to all this trouble when you have the guy in custody?"

Frank muttered, "Classified."

Harold interjected, "Relax, Frank. Bill, nothing's changed. We still need to understand why Chuck has gone through all of this trouble. There could be more lives at stake than our own."

"Like we talked about with Alice?"

"Exactly."

Bill continued, "But you don't think Chuck will give up who's directing him, or why?"

"Right again."

"Then why are you letting them use your yacht?"

Harold shrugged, "Maybe they can turn Chuck. I've been wrong before."

The sound of a Kodiak caught Bill's attention. Bill looked out towards the aft of the ship. Chuck stood up inside the bouncing craft, letting his legs absorb the shifting raft beneath him. Large handcuffs that appeared to be made from one piece of metal kept his wrists bound. Darla and Garcia sat with their submachine guns aimed at his back. A naval seaman navigated the craft, and another one sat at the bow facing the rest of the boat with a rifle pointed up in his hands.

Frank threw a rope to the seaman who quickly tied off the boat. Frank bounded up the stairs and put himself between Harold and the ladder. Darla stepped off next. She walked up the ladder and retrained her gun on Chuck. Chuck disembarked and stopped on the dive deck.

He looked up at Harold, "Permission to come aboard?"

"Granted."

Chuck responded, "Nice tub."

There was a tense silence.

Chuck said, "Isn't anyone going to help me up this ladder?"

Garcia left the Kodiak, and the craft departed. Garcia roughly pushed Chuck up the ladder.

Chuck looked towards Bill at the bar. "Hey, Billy. Come on over and join the party."

Bill answered, "Thanks, I like the smell better over here."

Chuck shrugged, "Suit yourself. Garcia's had a hard day. He can't help it if he sweats."

Garcia grabbed Chuck's arm, "Let's go, funnyman. You can joke all you like in your cabin."

Chuck looked over at Harold, "A cabin, just for me? You shouldn't have. By the way, I like your style. I refurbished an old military vessel for my operation base. She isn't nearly as beautiful on the outside, but she is all posh inside. We'll see if your taste can measure up."

Garcia yanked on Chuck's arm, and Chuck stumbled. "Let's go."

Garcia gave Darla his gun, and she shouldered the weapon and fell in behind Chuck while Garcia led the way inside.

Bill turned to Harold, "I hope you know what you're doing. Joshua is sure he's a berserker, and I don't think your ship can handle that kind of abuse."

Harold waved him off, "Don't worry. Garcia had a special room made just for Chuck in the hold of the ship."

"How do you know it can hold him?"

"I tested it."

Carol exited the interior, "What's all the commotion?"

Bill answered, "Chuck's onboard."

Carol's jawline drew tight, "What? I thought we left him behind for a reason."

Harold sat down on the couch, and Carol walked over and sat next to Bill at the bar.

Bill asked, "Do you want a beer?"

"Definitely," answered Carol.

"The good stuff is behind the bar in the fridge." Offered Harold.

Bill went behind the bar and found the refrigerator underneath stocked with Olde Meck. He pulled up a bottle and pointed at Harold, but Harold shook his head no. Bill rejoined Carol after opening up her bottle.

Carol said, "So, somebody tried to kill Chuck, and you bring the guy on the yacht? You don't think a lot for smart boys. Whoever is after Chuck will find this boat. It's not like it's hard to find a gleaming white yacht on the ocean."

"First, she's a ship."

Carol interrupted, "She. Why are boats and cars always women with you men."

Bill spoke up, "Because we love them."

Carol rolled her eyes, "Ah, ain't that sweet." She turned to Harold, "Your girlfriend is gonna get blown up."

Garcia and Darla reappeared.

Harold asked, "Is our guest happy with his accommodations?"

Darla answered, "Happy enough. He said it's the first real bed he's had to sleep on in weeks. I'm beginning to think we are going through a lot of trouble to turn somebody who's already turned.

Garcia said, "We need to stay on our toes. This is still Chuck. He could be playing us as much as we're playing him. I'm afraid Joshua and I will still need to have a heart to heart with Chuck to see if he's had a true change of heart."

Bill said, "The more you talk, the more this is sounding like torture."

Garcia asked, "Who said anything about torture. Harold?"

Harold held up his hands, "Don't look at me, I already told him that wasn't happening on my ship."

Darla looked Bill in the eyes as she spoke, "We would never torture Chuck. You can do a lot of things to someone mentally to break down their barriers. Some are pleasant, some aren't. None of the techniques are meant to cause any permanent damage."

Bill scowled, "That sounds like a polite way to say we'll only torture him if he forces us."

Garcia spoke up, "Were you ever afraid of the dark as a kid?"

Bill answered, "Sure, all kids are at some point."

Garcia nodded, "Were you in any real danger?"

Bill said, "No."

"That's all we're talking about here. We figure out Chuck's fears and make him assume his fears are going to come true if he doesn't cooperate."

"What if he lies about his fears?"

Garcia said, "That's why we have Joshua. Drugs can only work so well. Joshua can use hypnosis for diving deeper into his subconscious and finding out what Chuck is really after, and what he fears."

Harold asked, "I thought hypnosis only worked on people who allowed themselves to be hypnotized."

Darla responded, "The drugs will make Chuck more receptive to the idea."

Carol asked, "Will I be able to speak to Chuck?"

Bill interjected, "Yea, I want a word with him too."

Garcia said, "We'll see. Now, I would like everyone to go get their swim trunks on. We are having a farewell party to Alice on the top deck in 30 minutes. Please, be on time."

Bill looked at Harold and back at Garcia. "How can you be so cavalier? You didn't even bother to tell us she died, just show up for a farewell party?"

Darla answered, "Bill, this is harder for us than you think. Please, let us deal with things our way."

Harold asked, "What about Doc and Maria?"

Garcia answered, "I'll let them know."

CHAPTER 24

Bill's foot hung on his bathing suit, and he fell against the wall. Somebody knocked.

Bill yelled, "Who is it?"

"It's Harold."

Bill's lips buzzed as he blew out a lung full of air. He knocked the side of his head against the wall, pulled up his swim trunks, pushed himself off the wall, walked over to the door, and opened it.

Harold stood there in his Hawaiian teal swim trucks, a polo, and flip-flops. He pointed at the white stripe on his wrist, "Come on, man, we need to get topside."

Bill scowled and walked away to put on his shirt. "I thought we had thirty-minutes."

Harold said, "That's twenty-five minutes CIA time, and this is important, so I'm guessing we should be there in twenty."

Bill slipped on his flip flops. "Sorry, I didn't know."

Harold slapped him on the back as Bill exited his room. "It's alright. I was always late too."

The brothers made their way to the third deck. They found Darla and Garcia leaning against the bar with their sunglasses on. Darla had on a wrap over her bikini, and

Garcia had on a teal Bermuda swimsuit with prints of yellow surfers, a black t-shirt, and flip-flops.

Bill heard footsteps behind him as he and Harold made their way to the bar. Joshua and Maria topped the stairs. Maria's eyes were red and puffy. As soon as Joshua joined her on deck, she wrapped her arm tightly around his waist, and the two of them slowly walked towards the others.

Garcia moved behind the bar and pulled up a bottle of Scotch.

He said, "This is more than fifty years old. I was saving it for a special occasion, and this seems appropriate."

He filled each of the shot glasses and then lifted his. "This first drink is for Alice. She was one of the toughest women I ever knew, a good friend and a great boss."

Garcia rapped the bottom of the glass on the bar. Everyone followed his example. Garcia and Darla walked to the yacht's aft and poured their shots over the side. Bill, Harold, and the others followed suit. Everyone rejoined Garcia at the bar.

He poured another round and tapped and then raised his glass. Everyone joined in. Garcia said, "To a successful mission. Alice did not die in vain."

He downed his shot, and everyone followed suit. The liquor was smooth and warmed the back of Bill's throat. The warmth wrapped around his body down to his toes.

Garcia poured one more shot and put away the bottle. Bill noticed Garcia drank half his small glass and took that as a queue that the toasts were over. He took a sip and then sat down on the nearby barstool.

Bill watched the group make small talk. Darla pulled Maria aside, and Harold and Joshua began to debate the pros and cons of the Caribbean versus the west coast. A hand touched his arm. Carol's sleek dark body looked stunning beneath the white bikini she was wearing.

She cleared her throat, "My eyes are up here."

Bill felt his face flush. "Sorry. I just, well, you look amazing."

Carol smiled, and Bill detected a slight twinkle in her eyes. "I'm glad I can set your mind on happier things."

"I'm sorry you missed the ceremony. It was short. Garcia toasted to Alice's memory and then the mission."

Carol's lips went flat, "Yea, they told me thirty minutes. What's up with that?"

Bill put his hands on Carol's shoulders, and for a moment, he felt his fingers tingle. "It's not personal. I was under the same impression until Harold came and got me."

Carol's brow wrinkled, "And you're too busy for the woman you saved?"

Before he could stop himself, Bill cupped Carol's cheeks between his hands and looked deeply into her eyes. She returned his gaze.

A twinge of regret pierced his chest, and he dropped his hands. "I'm sorry. I mean, I don't know what's coming over me."

Carol replied, "Don't worry about it. I don't work for you anymore."

Bill's eyebrows went up, and his chest relaxed. His fingers gently caressed the outside of her arms.

Carol put her hand up, "Easy, boy. You ain't getting any of this," she waved across her body, "without some kind of commitment. Talk to the hand until we are out of this mess."

Bill's gaze passed down to the deck. Carol's cool hand lifted his chin, and she said, "Look at me. I'm not going anywhere anytime soon." She nodded to the nearby group. "I don't know if this is your family, friends, or strangers. I don't think you know either. Until we are back in Charlotte, we had better pay attention to more than just each other."

Bill nodded. "Alright."

Carol asked, "So, why did I get dissed?"

"Harold said it was CIA time. Evidently, thirty minutes means twenty-five. Harold said he thought this would be a twenty-minute waiting period because it was important. We started about ten minutes early.

"I would have gotten you, but Harold practically dragged me out of my cabin while I was still getting my clothes on."

Carol nodded, "Uh-huh. Well, I hate to think Chuck gave me more attention than the good guys."

Bill scowled, "How much attention."

Carol reached over and finished off Bill's shot. After she took a breath, she said, "Nice Scotch. As for Mr. McGill, you need to cool your jets, cowboy. If we are going anywhere, you have to trust me."

"I don't trust Chuck."

Carol leaned against his shoulder, "Okay. He never tried anything. He had a lot of questions about you. It was weird, though. He didn't ask about money or your career. He just wanted to know if I had any knowledge of your relationship with Harold.

"Then he asked me about your relationship with Lori and if you two were happy together."

Bill asked, "What did you tell him?"

"The truth. You two were happy. I told him Lori didn't seem like a gold digger, and the two of your made each other happy."

"What did Chuck say?"

Carol responded, "Nothing. He just got quiet, put out his cigar, stood up, and walked out of my room."

Garcia walked up, "Excuse me. I hate to intrude, but I need to talk to Bill."

"Come on, she just got away, and we would like to catch up."

Garcia put up his hands. "Alright, it's just a request. Do me a favor and don't leave the party. I want to have a chat before we shut down for tonight."

Bill nodded, and Garcia walked away.

Carol whispered, "What do you think he wants?"

Bill spoke softly, "I'm guessing it's about today and me causing Alice's death."

Carol scowled, "You did no such thing."

"Well, I think I did. She felt like she had to pull me aside after I tried to kill Chuck. If I had just played along, we probably would have been alright, and maybe Alice would have noticed the drone sooner or had been in a better position to hide from it."

Carol crossed her arms. "I swear, you sound so foolish sometimes. You did what you had to do to make sure I was safe. I know inside you want Chuck dead for what happened to Lori, but it wasn't like you started something. The man was taking potshots at us."

Bill answered, "Well, if it hadn't been for Darla, things would have ended differently, at least for Chuck. I know you want to believe I'm always in control, but I have to be honest with somebody. Something inside me wishes for bad things to come my way sometimes. I was happy when Chuck shot at us."

Carol's eyes widened.

Bill continued, "I was hoping he would start something. This thing inside me wanted out. It needed out."

"You make it sound like you keep him caged up. Like it's a whole other person living inside you. How is that any different than what Joshua did?"

Bill responded, "That's how it feels. It's just, I'm not sure how long I can keep this up. I mean, what if I spend my life looking for trouble? We both know that's a good way to end up dead or in prison."

Carol said, "Maybe you should stop treating that part of you like it's somebody else. It's who you are. You aren't any more evil or good than the rest of us. Didn't you ever hear a preacher say God's grace is sufficient?"

"Yea, that was usually right after telling everyone how bad they really are."

Carol scowled, "Don't be such a cynic."

"Right now, being a cynic seems to fit my life."

Carol waved her hand at him, "Whatever, listen to me. Those preachers were trying to say that Jesus' blood and the Holy Spirit can take what is bad and make it good. You've proven that multiple times already. You saved us at the office, you saved Darla at the airplane hangar, and you saved me today."

Bill asked, "How did you know about the hanger?"

"Chuck told me. He was complaining about the manpower you cost him."

Bill smiled and muttered, "Good."

Carol continued, "Don't get me off-topic. You need to focus on the good you can do and stop trying to pretend you're turning into something bad. This berserker, or whatever you guys call it, is you. Your strength, your bravery, it's a gift. What you do with it is up to you."

Bill looked skyward, "I would have preferred a family over any of this."

Carol grabbed his chin and pulled his face down so he looked into her eyes. His heart melted at the sight of her glistening eyes looking into his soul.

Carol said, "You need to stop living in the past. Look around you. This may be your family, but you're too busy wishing for something that didn't happen the way you wanted to notice."

Over from the other side of the deck, Harold announced, "I hate to be the party pooper, but it's time to end the party. Garcia, Darla, and Joshua have a big day tomorrow."

Garcia walked straight over to Bill and said, "Please don't go anywhere."

Carol hollered over to Harold, "I thought this was a pool party."

Harold shrugged and responded, "You never know when one might breakout. Maybe next time."

Darla answered, "It's just an excuse for the men to see us in our suits."

Maria added, "Boys."

Bill watched Joshua blush while Harold's smile was barely perceptible under his red beard. Everyone began to leave except Garcia. Carol gave Bill a hug and headed down with the rest of the group.

Garcia said, "Please, join me in the hot tub."

CHAPTER 25

Bill felt the hot water wash over his sore muscles. He gasped as his waist slipped below the waterline. The hot liquid and air jets relaxed the day's tension and soreness. Bill closed his eyes, laid his head back on the deck, and struggled to stay awake.

Garcia's voice was barely perceptible over the sound of the water jets. "Stay with me, Bill. You can relax after we talk."

Visions of the day's events at the island came rushing into Bill's mind, and he sat up. The evening air blew against his tired chest and shoulders.

"I'm sorry."

Garcia asked, "For what?"

Bill could feel the tears pooling in his eyes. "If I hadn't acted out, Alice might still be alive."

Garcia reached over and squeezed Bill's shoulder. "That wasn't your fault. Alice was in a position to shoot down the drone. Whoever operated the craft had her in their crosshairs before she squeezed her trigger.

"I'm actually more concerned with your reaction to Chuck. How can I know you won't kill him if I let you talk with him?"

Bill looked up at the darkening sky. "I don't know. I mean, I want to say I won't, but what if he tries something? I know deep down inside I want him to try something so I can kill him.

"Everybody keeps giving me advice about the new me, but I'm not sure anyone really understands."

Garcia propped his elbows on the deck and checked his watch. He held up his finger, "Hold that thought."

Frank appeared from the stairs with four rum runners. He put two down for each of them and then left."

Bill said, "I'm not a heavy drinker."

Garcia smiled, "Neither am I. Consider these virgins, well, almost virgins."

Bill took a swallow, and the fruit juices wash over his throat in a cold, sweet liquid with just a hint of rum.

Garcia put down his glass, let out a sigh and said, "This isn't a new you. It's who you are. I understand you had this vision of yourself as a quiet, everyday guy who worked in finance. You're still that guy."

Bill interrupted, "I'm still that guy even though I killed five people?"

Garcia nodded, "True. Taking a life does change you, but how you chose to react to it comes from your heart. I'm probably one of the few people that can understand how you feel. I know what it feels like to do something you never thought you were capable of doing."

"Please tell me it's not that coffee story about your dad that Harold warned me about."

Garcia scowled, "No. This story is about me during the second gulf war. I've never shared this with anyone.

"I volunteered to slip into Syria. We knew there were terrorist camps, ties to smaller groups, and some of those had ties to Al Qaeda. My assignment was to find any leaders, report my findings, and if possible, eliminate the targets."

Bill's eyes widened, "You were an assassin?"

Garcia replied, "A soldier, we were at war."

"But you work for the CIA?"

Garcia took a sip of his drink and then said, "Remember, this is classified."

Bill nodded.

Garcia continued, "I was on the outskirts of a small eastern Syrian village. Do you remember John the Baptist from the Bible? The guy who ate locust and honey?"

"Yea,"

Garcia said, "Well, I was living on MREs and bugs. I had crawled around so long in the dirt I thought I was going to turn into a snake. We had good intel on a leader trying to create a new cell called ISIS. It was early, so taking out anyone could collapse their effort.

"There was a shepherd who could come and go from the town without question. He had no love for the men who had invaded his village. The terrorists had taken many of the younger girls and put them in a building where the men stayed. Pedophilia is big with these guys."

Bill scowled, squeezed his glass, and finished off his first drink.

Garcia kept talking, "The shepherd told me an Al Qaeda leader was coming to town to meet with the leader of the terrorist cell. With us taking Afghanistan, Iraq's collapse, and Syria's government in shambles, they thought they could move part of their operation to Syria.

"The building where they stayed was in the middle of town, but I was lucky because the meeting was supposed to happen in the middle of the night. As soon as it got dark, I made my way to the edge of the village. The shepherd's family hid me in their house and gave me some clothes to wear to blend in better. I used their home as my new base of operation until it was time for the meeting.

"My plan was to scout the building where the terrorists were meeting. I would confirm who was there and then paint the building's side for our bombers. When I arrived at the end of their street, I knew I had a problem. The terrorist had planned their location well. There was an apartment building across the street, a clinic with a small section for overnight patients next door, and several residences.

"I moved in closer to see how many people were in the nearby buildings. As I walked down the street, I could hear the girls screaming from inside the terrorists' structure. A young boy sat next to the entrance of the terrorists' house with a blanket over himself, huddled up crying.

"A guard approached me and told me to get away, so I hurried down the block and slipped out of sight. I had a choice to make. If I called in the bombing and took the terrorists out, it would also kill the children being raped inside. It might also kill some civilians in the surrounding buildings. I still didn't have any ids, but I had enough. If I did nothing, the nightmare would continue for the kids, and the terrorists would completely take over the town once Al Qaeda agreed to join them."

Garcia finished his second glass. "The screaming of adults replaced the screaming of children. We dropped one five-hundred-pound bomb on target. The clinic received some damage, but fortunately, those beds were empty. The apartment building was old, and the shock-wave caused a partial collapse. Three residents perished, but the rest were rescued."

Bill asked, "What about the terrorists and kids?"

Garcia watched his fingers as they played against the bubbles in the water, "Nobody survived in the house."

Both men sat there quietly. The jets turned off, and Bill pushed himself out and sat on the edge of the hot tub with his legs dangling in the water. Garcia followed suit.

Garcia said, "You know, at first I told myself I was a hero. At least that's what everyone else told me, so I believed it to make myself feel better. But, at night, when I was alone in my bed, I could still hear the screaming. I finally had to face the fact that I had caused the deaths of innocent people."

Bill interrupted, "They weren't innocent. They were terrorists."

Garcia looked into Bill's eyes, "And some were children, rape victims, mothers and fathers in bed with their families thinking they were safe. I started to question whether I was as much of a terrorist as the people I was hunting."

Bill said, "That's not you."

"You're right. That's not who I am. I analyzed everything about that mission for months. If I had walked away, things would have been worse, not only for the villagers but the surrounding area. I realized that sometimes we don't have a choice between good and evil. Sometimes, the option is about the best long-term outcome to an already bad situation. I wanted to shorten the suffering, even though I temporarily added to it.

"That experience brought me to God and Jesus."

Bill asked, "Blowing people up brought you to Jesus?"

Garcia's mouth curved down slightly. "No. the need for forgiveness brought me to him. It doesn't matter how good your reasons are for killing someone; it's not our right to take somebody's life. However, some of us are created to do that so that others don't die.

"The feeling of taking innocent lives was still more than I could handle. So, I started reading the Bible. I had remembered some stories I heard during mass as a kid. I read about David and Sampson. I saw how God used them and gave them grace because God had put them on earth to do brutal, violent acts to save Israel.

"If God is the same no matter the century, and if Jesus really brought about forgiveness for all humanity, then it made sense that all of that would apply to me."

Bill put up his hands, "Okay, you can stop there. We attended church every Sunday and had daily devotions at the orphanage. I have to be honest. I have yet to see any evidence of God.

"I asked for parents. I believed for parents and got nothing. If He exists, where's the family? Not only that, God let Lori and our baby be murdered. I have yet to see evidence from this God I was raised on."

Garcia answered, "Let me leave you with this thought. Are you missing God because he's not answering the way you think He should answer, or is it because He's done nothing in your life?"

"Oh, He's done something alright. He's given me this raging personality that can make bashing in skulls seems as enjoyable as a day at the beach."

Garcia said, "So, you do believe God exists."

Bill scowled.

Garcia grabbed his towel and stood up. He looked down at Bill and said, "Just think about what we've talked about. You have a brother who loves you. Joshua thinks of you as a son. Evidently, Carol is interested in being more than just a friend if body language is any indicator. Don't destroy the blessings in front of you for the darkness around you."

Garcia turned on his heel and headed down the stairs without saying goodnight. Bill lifted his legs out of the water and laid on his back. The stars formed a canopy across the black sky. The cold ocean breeze washed over his body, and he threw his towel over himself to stay warm.

Bill spoke to the night, "If you're there, could you give me some sort of sign? I only see death, lies, and secrets. I just want to know I'm going to be alright, and I'm not alone."

Carol's familiar voice spoke from across the deck at the stairwell. "You're not alone, baby."

She cleared the top of the steps. Bill could see she had changed into a pair of black shorts and a white t-shirt. Bill had a tough time taking his eyes off her.

Carol laid down next to Bill, "You can blink now."

Bill stammered.

Carol laughed.

Bill asked, "How did you know I'd be here still?"

"Let's just say a little spy told me."

Bill slipped his arm around Carol and threw the towel over her. The warmth of their bodies made Bill sleepy. He could feel himself relaxing.

Carol whispered near his ear, "Don't give up the faith. Your life is not about death. It's about living."

Bill sat up, "What? Why did you say that?"

Carol's eyes widened, "What's wrong?"

"Did you hear me praying?" demanded Bill.

Carol answered, "No, I just heard you ask God to tell you that you aren't alone."

Bill rubbed his face in the palm of his hands. He asked, "What made you say my life isn't about death?"

Carol took his hands, "I thought you might still be upset about Alice, and something inside me told me to say it."

Bill hugged her. She smelled like a field of flowers, and Bill nestled his face into the crook of her neck, and before he could stop himself, he let his lips gently kiss her silky dark skin. He released Carol and sat up.

Bill said, "I, uh, I'm sorry. I don't know what, um."

Carol interrupted, "It's alright."

Bill kissed her fingers and then stood up and offered Carol his hand. She held it and raised herself off the deck. The two held hands down to their cabins. They hugged goodnight and went into their separate rooms. Bill turned on the satellite television and stared blankly at the weather channel.

CHAPTER 26

Bill stood alone in the familiar woods clothed in wolfskin. The trees shuddered with a howl. He reached for his weapons, but they were absent.

He spoke to himself, "This is just a dream. Concentrate, you can wake up."

The howl grew louder and more desperate.

"Wake up, come on, wake up!"

Bill's eyes shot open. A roar through the walls made the pictures and television around the cabin vibrate. He rolled out of bed and grabbed some clothes. Another howl came through, but this one sounded more distant.

Bill opened his cabin door and looked up and down the hall. There was nobody to be seen. He ran for the stairs and up to the main deck. The ship still appeared deserted. He topped the stairs and quickly maneuvered around the indoor dining table and into the living room.

Bill stopped and looked through the sliding glass door. Maria, Darla, Harold, and Carol all sat at the round dining table with their morning meals. Maria had a scowl on her face, uninterested in the food. Harold had shaved his beard and cut his hair. To Bill, his brother now looked more like the man he had seen in the business magazines.

Bill rushed over and opened the door. "What's going on?"

Darla and Harold looked up, "Good morning."

Maria and Carol did not make eye contact.

Bill asked again, "Hey, what's going on?"

Darla answered, "What do you mean?"

Bill scowled, "I thought I heard Harold holler, you know like something was wrong. I come up here, and everyone is having quiet breakfast."

Darla said, "Joshua and Garcia are questioning Chuck." She took a bite of eggs.

Maria spoke up, "You mean torturing him. I know what that sounds like. Men from the cartel used to enter my village and "question" a family about talking to the police. I can still hear their screams."

Harold asked, "Maria, do you know who gave those cartel men their weapons and who told them when someone in a village had betrayed them?"

Maria shook her head.

Harold answered, "Men like Chuck. They make money on the misery of others. If they can create a conflict to sell more goods to a customer, they'll do it every time. That's not the villagers you hear screaming down there. It's the cartel."

Maria crossed her arms, "Joshua told me he wouldn't torture anyone."

Darla answered, "He's not torturing him. Garcia and Joshua are making Chuck review where he has been, his victims, who paid him to do the things he did. Anybody with Chuck's past is going to have his demons to face."

Harold shook his head. "I don't know. Chuck's a smart guy. I trust the Doc, but I hope the information they're getting is reliable."

Darla grabbed Harold's wrist, "They know what they're doing."

Bill asked, "How long have they been at it?"

Darla answered, "About an hour."

Bill looked over at the clock over the bar, "I slept in this late, with that going on?"

Darla answered, "Garcia gave you a mild sedative in your drink last night so you would be able to sleep."

Bill scowled, "Thanks for asking. Well, I'll be back up in fifteen minutes. I'd like some breakfast."

Harold answered, "No problem."

Bill sulked over Garcia's actions as he made his way back to his cabin. He slipped off his clothes, got in a shower amidst the chorus of howls echoing through the lower parts of the ship. When he returned for breakfast, Carol sat waiting for him.

"Where did the rest go?"

Carol answered, "Darla and Harold said they will be back soon. Something about checking on the Doc and Garcia. Maria is upstairs. She said she wanted to get away from the noise."

Bill sat down, "I can't really hear much of anything up here."

Frank appeared with eggs, bacon, and a large mug of coffee. Bill savored his first sip of coffee and the perfectly cooked breakfast.

Carol asked, "Are you alright with what's going on?"

Bill put down his fork, "What do you mean?"

"This Chuck guy. Do you think he's really as bad as they say, or are you just taking their word for it?"

Bill scowled, "He killed Lori, he tried to kidnap me, and he almost made you a sex slave."

"I know, but why not just throw him in prison? This seems cruel."

Bill answered, "No crueler than he was to us."

"That's what I mean. We aren't supposed to be like him. Didn't you ever learn that two wrongs don't make a right?"

Bill nodded. "This isn't that simple, at least from what I've heard. It sounds like they can stop a lot of bad people if they can get Chuck to talk to them."

"Maybe they should just ask him."

Bill picked up his fork, "I don't think Chuck's honesty is worth much."

Carol looked out over the sea as Bill quickly finished his breakfast. He was getting down his last bite when Harold and Darla emerged.

Carol asked, "Is he still alive?"

Darla answered, "Yes. He's been giving the guys lots of good intel."

Carol's eyes narrowed, "And what are the guys giving him?"

Darla and Harold joined them at the table as Frank showed up with a coffee decanter.

Harold answered, "Doc has been helping Chuck work through the people he killed. The howling we're hearing is a combination of him reliving the events and grief."

Bill asked, "And Chuck's okay with that?"

Darla answered, "Garcia was going to stop when they got the name of the person behind this operation, but Chuck asked him if Doc could help him face his demons."

Bill said, "Wait, you have the answer? Who is it?"

Darla put up her hand, "Just wait. We'll have a debrief with everyone in a little while. Joshua wants to finish with Chuck and see where things are. Garcia thinks they're turning him."

Carol asked, "Turning him into what?"

Darla answered, "Turning him to our side."

Bill noticed a slight shake of Harold's head. He asked, "You don't agree with your wife?"

Harold answered, "Chuck's a smart guy. Doc is smart too, but I'm afraid he's letting Garcia's optimism get the better of him."

Darla said, "Darling, I can't believe you'd say that about your mentor."

Harold answered, "Doc is family, and I'd say that about my own dad if somebody was trying to take advantage of him."

Darla answered, "Well, you'll get your chance soon enough. Joshua said he thought it would be safe if you and Bill went in together to talk to Chuck. We're going to see if we can learn anything new when he talks with both of you."

Bill asked, "When?"

Darla answered, "As soon as the two of them return. It could be in a few minutes or a few hours. In the meantime, I suggest we change the subjects or do something to pass the time."

Bill turned to Harold, "So, where's your lion's mane?"

Harold blushed, "Well, it's going to sound a little crazy. When Chuck got away, I made a vow to God that I wouldn't shave until we caught him or killed him."

"We know," interrupted Bill.

Darla rolled her eyes, "You're still going with that? Just admit it. You called it a "vow" so Garcia and I would find him faster. That beard was hideous."

Harold laughed, "The vow was real, but it did have some side benefits. I saved a lot of time not shaving."

Carol asked, "Has anyone seen Maria recently? The last time I saw her, she was going to the top deck."

Darla answered, "She took the elevator down. I saw her in the hall, she said she was going to pray for everybody."

Carol responded, "Smart woman."

"This thing has an elevator?" asked Bill.

Harold nodded, "CIA had it installed in case they needed to transport wounded agents. It's used by the staff most of the time now."

Bill answered, "But your staff is CIA.

"If you'll excuse me, I think I'll go for a short walk."

Carol stood to join him. The two went to the third deck and walked forward to the front of the ship. The salt breeze blew past them. There were no sounds of screaming or people bickering about what was going on.

Carol slid her arm around his and put her head on his shoulder. He slid his fingers between her's and gave her a light kiss on the back of her hand.

He whispered, "Thank you for being such a good friend."

Ahead of the ship, he could see the Bahamas' minor island chains. They were not far from Cuba, but far enough. The dot of a small vessel on the port side seemed to match their speed.

Bill pointed out towards the horizon and asked, "Do you see a small black dot out there, or am I seeing things?"

Carol stared for several seconds and finally answered, "That's a ship or something. Do you think we should tell somebody?"

Bill let go of Carol's hand. "Let's head downstairs and ask Darla."

The two went back down to find Darla asleep against Harold's broad shoulder. Harold gently pushed against her head when Bill and Carol came closer.

Bill asked, "Did you know a ship is shadowing us?"

Darla yawned, stretched, and then asked, "Is it on the port side?"

Carol asked, "What side is that?"

Harold answered, "The left side."

Carol said, "No, the right."

Darla smiled and laid her head back on Harold's shoulder, and said, "Good, it's one of ours. It's just escorting us until Chuck is off the ship."

Bill commented, "It seems pretty far away."

Darla mumbled, "Don't worry, the navy knows what it's doing."

Bill looked at Carol. Her look was as skeptical as he felt. The sliding glass door opened, and Garcia emerged.

He pointed at Harold and Bill. Alright, you two, you wanted to talk to Chuck; here's your chance. His only requirement is that he talks to both of you alone. Don't worry. The room is wired for sound and video. I'm sure Chuck knows that. He's just being Chuck.

Bill asked, "So, you won't be in there?"

Garcia answered, "No."

Harold asked, "What about Doc?"

Garcia answered, "We're right outside the door."

Bill said, "Okay. I've been waiting for this. Let's go."

Garcia stepped in front of Bill, "You and Harold follow me."

The three men began their journey into the bottom of the ship.

CHAPTER 27

The steel was painted white. Unlike the yacht's luxurious parts, this was nothing more than bracing, plating, and rivets. A small room straddled the keel. It looked like a cube dropped into the bottom of the ship. Harold ducked to enter, and Bill felt his hair brush the top of the door frame. The ceiling lightly touched the top of Harold's hair.

Bill had never been claustrophobic, but the low ceiling and ten-by-ten room made him nervous. Chuck was chained to a desk that was welded to the floor. He chewed on an unlit cigar that he clenched between his teeth.

Chuck smiled and said, "I'd stand up, but I'm afraid that isn't possible at the moment. Please, have a seat, boys."

Garcia spoke up, "I'll be right outside."

Chuck nodded, and Garcia left the room and closed the door.

Harold commented, "I'm surprised Doc wasn't still in here with you."

Chuck shrugged, "He's around here somewhere. I imagine Garcia has him monitoring me on the cameras they tried to hide behind the walls." Chuck gazed around the room, "I can't see them, but I know they're here."

Bill asked, "Why did you have Lori killed?"

Chuck turned and looked at Bill. His dead eyes put a chill down Bill's spine. Chuck's lips curled down. He said, "I didn't have Lori killed. I thought you understood that."

Bill leaned closer, despite the fear that was twinging in his back. He said, "You sent Nigel to get me. He killed Lori, so you had Lori killed. Why? Why even come for me? I had nothing to do with any of this. Your song and dance about revenge, and then a mysterious stranger wanting to meet my brother doesn't hold water with me. Men like you do what they want, and you want what benefits you."

Chuck's lips stayed flat. He pulled out his cigar, spat on the floor, and stuck it back in.

Harold said, "Well, answer my brother. I want to know the answer too."

Chuck looked down at the desk. "It has to do with Harold's father."

Harold raised his voice, "My father's dead."

Chuck shook his head, "No, your real father."

Harold stood and hovered over Chuck. Bill pushed his chair out of the way. Harold growled, "My real father is dead," and then sat back down.

Bill asked, "Harold's Uncle did this?"

Chuck pointed at Bill. "You really are the smart one. Yes, Harold's father is behind all of this."

Harold spoke up, "Okay, first of all, he's not my father. He's a rapist and a sperm donor who has nothing to do with me. Secondly, you expect us to believe that an estranged relative who raped my mom suddenly decides to come after me decades later? How does that even make sense?"

Chuck pushed back against his chair and took the cigar out of his mouth. "The man who helped conceive you is named Hunter. He has been searching for you ever since your mother put you in an orphanage. Garcia won't tell me how they did it. Still, somehow your mom, April, Rachel, or whatever she was calling herself then, and the orphanage managed to conceal your identity when you were adopted.

"Hunter found out who your parents were a few years ago. He knew you wouldn't have anything to do with him now that you're a grown man. So, I was asked to execute a plan that would cause your father to be desperate to do business with him. His plan was to work his way into your family, become your friend, and then reveal who he really is."

Bill spoke up, "That sounds nuts. What kind of a loon does that? Who is this guy?"

Chuck looked back at Bill, "He may be a loon, but he's a smart loon.

"Hunter ran into a guy from Yemen while in hiding. Hunter's new friend got him in touch with some freedom fighters in the middle east."

Harold interrupted, "You mean terrorists."

Chuck smiled, "It depends on which side you're on. Anyway, Hunter found a group of men he could get along with. They appreciated his fighting ability, and he appreciated their views on women and other vices."

Bill interrupted, "Wait if he's hanging out with Muslim extremists, wouldn't they believe the opposite of what Hunter would want?"

Chuck laughed for a moment and then started to chew on his cigar again. "Kid, you have so much to learn about the world. These guys aren't practicing Muslims. That just gives them cover. Sure, there are a few real believers in their ranks to make them look legit. Most of these guys are just warlords looking for their piece of the pie.

"Anyway, Hunter got his piece of the pie. He runs a small village in the middle of Iran. Hunter provides men to Iran for certain missions with weapons from me. The Iranian government leaves him alone to govern his village as he sees fit, as long as he's at their disposal."

Bill said, "It sounds like he has a village full of slaves."

Chuck shook his head, "No, you have it all wrong. These are volunteers. They are berserkers, like you two. They're people who struggled with their gift in the civilized world, so Hunter gave them what they really wanted. A place to practice their talent. Skirmishes and wars to fight to their heart's content."

Harold asked, "I still don't understand. Why come after me, or Bill?"

Chuck answered, "Because you're Hunter's son. He's planning to pass the torch to you. As for your half-brother, well, he was just the bait. Hunter doesn't allow half-breeds into the family."

Bill leaned forward, "What do you mean, half-breeds?"

Chuck lifted up his handcuffed hands, and the chains rattled, "Easy, that's just Hunter's words. Full-blooded berserkers only. He wants to keep the bloodline pure."

Bill commented, "Great, another bigot with delusions of grandeur."

Chuck shrugged, "Yea, well, it's working out for him so far. Anyway, we didn't know you were a berserker. Hunter assumed April had either jumped Joshua's bones or found some poor sap who liked crazy women."

Bill grumbled, "It was Hunter that made her crazy."

Chuck took out his cigar, "Yea, well, I wasn't there, so I can't say. If Hunter had realized your ability, I'm sure you'd make the recruitment list."

Bill shook his head, "Don't bother."

Harold asked, "So, why are you spilling the beans?"

Chuck answered, "I know when I'm beaten. Hunter put me on a timer after the sting operation to bring you in. He's pushing seventy, and his doctor told him after he turned sixty he could keel over at any time. So, he's desperate to meet his son and try to get you to take over the family business."

Harold quipped, "I already have a family business."

Chuck continued, "Nobody was supposed to get killed when I had Nigel come for Bill. My plan was to snatch your brother, make a trade, and deliver you to Hunter to work out your family issues. After that fiasco blew up in my face, I was out of men and had to find freelancers to help with everything. The episode at the hanger was another fiasco. They were supposed to take Bill while he was being transported to the airport, but these guys thought they knew better."

Harold asked, "What about Darla? She's not a berserker. What was Hunter's plan for my wife?"

Chuck answered, "He was going to take you without her. According to Hunter, he had a woman picked out that would make you forget all about Darla."

Harold rolled his eyes and then said, "This guy's an idiot. Do you know how to get in touch with him?"

Chuck answered, "Yea, Garcia is going to have me contact him once we get to Gitmo. You have a message for him?"

Harold leaned in close until he was almost touching the cigar in Chuck's mouth. He said, "Tell Hunter if I ever see him near me, my family, or my friends, I'll kill him."

Chuck smiled, "Noted."

Bill spoke up, "You can second that for me as well."

Chuck answered, "It sounds like the family reunion is postponed indefinitely."

Bill said, "I think we have some things to talk about."

"Then let's talk." Quipped Chuck.

Harold said, "He meant without you."

Chuck nodded.

Bill stood, and Harold followed suit. They knocked on the door, and Garcia let them out. The three men walked up the first ladder to the cabins in silence. Joshua came out of his room and joined them. The group headed up the next set of stairs to the main deck.

Darla looked up from the table, "Well?"

Bill answered, "I have a lot to think about."

Harold responded to her, "You and I can talk about it in our room."

Carol asked, "Is there anything I can do?"

Joshua interjected, "We can talk if you like."

Bill shook his head. "Just give me some time. I'm not sure I can explain what's going on in my head."

Everyone sat down. Harold continued the conversation. "Chuck told us about Hunter."

Darla and Garcia looked at each other and back to Harold and Bill. "Okay, we expected that."

Bill leaned towards Garcia, "What do you mean you expected that?"

Darla answered, "Chuck told us the same thing. Harold, you know Chuck as well as we do. He's going to say anything he can to get a rise out of both of you."

"So, then it's not true?" asked Bill.

Garcia answered, "Oh, I think it checks out. Bill, you were correct in your early observations. Chuck has no reason to have gone this far. He could have had a quiet retirement in some unwatched corner of the globe if somebody wasn't pushing his buttons."

Bill scowled, "Lori died for nothing."

Carol took Bill's hand, "No, she didn't."

Bill looked into her eyes. Carol's black eyes glistened, and a tear ran down her cheek. "She brought you back together with your brother."

Bill asked, "How?"

Carol responded, "If it wasn't for Chuck, Lori's death, and whoever this Hunter character is, you would have never found your brother."

Bill took his hand back and crossed his arms. He mumbled, "I'm not sure it was worth the trade." He looked over at Harold, "No offense."

"None taken," replied Harold.

Joshua spoke up, "I think Bill's right. Let's talk more about this tomorrow."

Bill stood, "I need some time alone. I'll be in my cabin."

He left everyone and locked the door to his room. Bill stared out the window and spoke. "So, this is it? This is how you answer my questions? I wanted a family, and you gave me a brother who already has a family. I ask you why Lori died, and you show me a psychopath."

Bill reached for a nearby book and flung it into the wall on the far side of the room. He let out a long, slow breath and then whispered, "You're the God of the universe. I expected something more meaningful."

Chapter 28

Bill's body awoke with a jolt. Alarm bells rang in the hall, and the lights in the cabin turned on, flickered, and then the room went dark. Emergency lights began to glow and gain strength along the floor and corners of the ceiling. Metal groaned, and the ship started to rock back and forth. Automatic gunfire merged with the alarm bells.

Bill stumbled out of bed and grabbed a pair of shorts. He opened his door to find Darla dashing towards the stairs. Carol crashed into Bill and held him tight. Harold ran up and pulled Carol off Bill.

Harold's breath was labored. He blinked, and his bloodshot eyes focused on Bill.

Harold growled, "Carol has to get topside and wait in the kitchen."

Carol's eyes widened, "You're crazy if you think I'm going up there."

Maria and Joshua ran up. Maria grabbed Carol's hand, "Stay with me."

Carol nodded, and the three hurried towards the stairs.

Harold's voice rumbled, "We have to keep an eye on Chuck."

Bill followed Harold to the hatch leading down to the bottom of the ship. The sound of water pouring in echoed behind the door.

Bill asked, "Is his door watertight?"

Harold sucked in a long, slow breath and held up his finger. He took a second breath, and his eyes cleared, "I don't know. I don't think so. Garcia didn't have us pump air into the cell."

Bill reached for the door, and Harold grabbed his hand. "What are you doing? You could flood the ship if the water gets high enough."

"We can't let him drown in there."

Harold shook his head, "No. If they can get the pumps online, he should be alright."

Bill protested, "I'm not like Chuck. I won't let him drown. Just be ready for us."

Harold let go of his brother's hand, and Bill tried to unlatch the bulkhead. It wouldn't budge. He beat on it, and his heartbeat began to drown out the echo of steel against his fist. He pushed up against the latch with his shoulder. The metal screamed and gave way.

He started inside the dark doorway, but Harold grabbed his shoulder.

He handed Bill a key and flashlight. "Here, it's an emergency light. The water won't put it out."

Bill nodded, grabbed it, and headed down the stairs. The cold seawater was up to his knees as he pushed his way towards the cell. The stench of diesel caused Bill to wretch. The flashlight appeared amber before his vision.

Bill beat on the door and hollered, "Are you alright?"

Chuck's faint voice hollered from the other side, "I'm handcuffed to the bed, and the water is rising. Get me out of here."

Bill fumbled with the key but managed to unlock the cell. The hatch bolts moaned, and Bill fought against the surging water. He threw his body against the door, and the top hinge broke loose. The door collapsed underneath Bill, and he tumbled into the water. Salt and oil saturated his mouth.

Bill pushed himself to his knees, spit, and then took a deep breath. A strike on his back turned from pleasure to pain. Bill closed his mouth as he went back under the water. Chuck's hand pressed down on the back of his head. Bill turned off the flashlight still in his hand.

Bill's free hand grappled in the dark until he grabbed Chuck's pinky. He twisted and pulled it to the side. Chuck roared, and Bill continued to rotate it. Chuck's hand slid off his head, and Bill planted his foot and thrust his body upwards.

He broke free of the water with the sound of Chuck tumbling underneath its surface. Bill switched on the flashlight and scanned the dark water for Chuck. His foot suddenly twisted, and he plummeted back under.

Bill turned the light towards his feet and saw Chuck scrambling to get some air. Bill kicked at Chuck, but the water fought against his strength, and Chuck broke away. A foot slammed down on Bill's neck, and Chuck twisted his shoe against Bill's skin. Bill turned off the flashlight again and tried to get free.

Chuck's strength was equal to his own, and Bill could feel his chest start to ache. Desperate, he grabbed Chuck's foot and managed to make him stumble back to attempt to regain his leverage. Bill pulled Chuck's ankle into his mouth. He bit down as hard as he could and pulled. Chuck's Achilles tendon snapped.

Bill could hear Chuck's roar above the water. Chuck's foot slid off his neck, and Bill pushed himself up. The sour air tasted good and refreshed Bill's lungs.

Chuck splashed around in the darkness and stammered, "Can't we call it a draw?"

Bill felt the flashlight bump against his foot and grabbed it. A pole lay under the water next to it. He grabbed both and turned on the flashlight.

Two arms wrapped around Bill's shins. Bill raised the bar, twisted his body, and slammed the pole against Chuck's skull. Dark liquid poured from the side of Chuck's head. His grip relaxed, and he rolled to his side. Bill leaned against the dank wall and worked to breathe. A pain pierced his rib, and then euphoria swept liked a wave across his chest.

Chuck's twisted smile barely appeared above the water. He held fast to the shank handle. The steel had pierced the skin, but it stopped against Bill's freshly broken rib. Bill wrestled for the shank and fell on top of Chuck. Their bodies rolled beneath the poisonous waters.

Chuck got on top and pinned Bill down. Bill could feel the tip of the shank against his sternum. Chuck's weight pressed down on the handle. In a desperate move, Bill flipped the blade around. Chuck lost his grip and fell on the blade.

Bill rolled Chuck off him and burst above the water. He hunted for his flashlight, grabbed hold of it and collapsed back into the water. He fought his way to his feet. Chuck floated in the water with blood pouring from his chest wound; his face frozen with a grimaced and bloodshot eyes.

Harold's voice echoed, "Are you okay?"

Bill tried to reply, but his lungs started to burn. The red beam began to turn amber and then pink. He leaned up against the wall and tried to maintain his footing. The water was up to Bill's thighs, and his muscles stung. He tried to focus on his breathing, but the foul air was making him lightheaded.

Bill grabbed the doorjamb and forced himself to take a step. His stomach cramped up and dirty water expelled from his mouth. The sound of someone bounding down the steps and the splashing of water swirled in Bill's mind. The light he had been following suddenly slipped beneath the surface of the surly water.

Another light appeared. Bill took a step towards it, stumbled, and felt the waves swallow his body. He tried to breathe, but putrid water filled his lungs. Something grabbed hold and raised him above the surface.

Harold's far away voice sounded worried, "Don't you leave me."

Bill squinted at the light as it turned dimmer. He tried to breathe again, but there was no room for air. A calm fell over his body, and the light faded from view.

CHAPTER 29

Bill sat in the red cushioned chair inside the administrator's office. His short legs swung back and forth. Bored, he started counting the boards on the floor, but the familiar sound of footsteps in the hall caused him to look up. The office door opened, and Joshua stood there with a smile on his face.

Joshua said, "Billy, I have a couple who would like to meet you. May they come in?"

Bill smiled, and he nodded vigorously. A man and woman walked in. He wore a navy-blue suit against his fit body. The man had thick, black wavy hair that he combed back. He was at least as tall as Joshua and looked like a giant to Bill. The woman reminded Bill of one of the porcelain dolls the girls in the orphanage played with. She was the most beautiful woman Bill had ever seen.

Bill slipped off his chair and attempted to straighten the suit that was too large for him. The woman kneeled and smiled, "I'm Barbara Brown, and this is my husband, Richard. We're your brother's parents. How would you like to come with us and live with your brother?"

Bill's eyes widened, "You mean like a forever family?"

Richard kneeled down next to his wife, "That's exactly what we mean."

Before Bill could stop himself, he hugged both of them. Then his vision faded.

He felt a pain in his chest, and the room came back into view. Tears streamed down his cheeks, and he could feel Joshua holding him in his lap. He was crying as well.

Bill blubbered, "Why? Why can't they adopt me? They said they love me."

Joshua rocked Bill back and forth. "I wish I could tell you. Your mom doesn't want to give up custody."

Bill felt his cheeks flush, "Then why isn't she here? Why doesn't she come to get me?"

Joshua said, "We need to pray God will reunite you with your mother."

Bill pushed himself off Joshua and slipped off his leg. He glared at Joshua and said, "Pray, what good will that do? If God cared, he would have given me to the Browns. This sucks, and so does God."

Bill ran out of the room and back into the darkness.

Bill and his new boss, Gerard, stood in front of his office. "Everyone, your attention, please. This is Bill Johnson. He's the new Investment Branch Manager. Bill was very successful with several large corporate clients while on Wall Street. We hope to see him bring the same success to everyone here in our little corner of Charlotte."

The workers politely clapped. Gerard waved over a beautiful African American woman.

Gerard introduced her. "Bill, this is Carol Lewis. She's your new administrator."

Bill stuck out his hand, "A pleasure."

Carol politely replied, "The pleasure is all mine."

Gerard continued, "She'll get you up to speed on things. You'll be lost without her, so keep her happy. If you two will excuse me, I have a noon flight back to London I need to catch."

They said their goodbyes. Carol took Bill into his office and showed him around. She bent over at a filing cabinet to show him where the personnel folders were kept. Bill couldn't help noticing how she filled out her dress.

Without looking at him, Carol said, "I'm glad you appreciate my booty, but I don't date my bosses."

Bill's face got warmer, and he stammered, "I was looking at the filing cabinet."

Carol stood up. "Uh-huh. Just so you know, that's a hard no."

Bill asked, "Are you always this blunt with your new bosses?"

Carol smiled, "Only the cute ones. Now come over to your desk, and let's get you logged into the system."

The office faded, another pain shot across his chest.

He sat with Lori at Capital Grille for lunch. They gazed into one another's eyes. Bill reached over and held her hand while he ran his thumb gently across her skin. Lori shivered and pulled her hand back.

"We need to slow down."

Bill smiled, "So, you feel it too?"

Lori cocked her head, "Feel what?"

Bill's grin spread across his face. "The electricity between us, but it's more than that. It feels like you've been beside me my whole life. It's like we've always known each other, but there's an unseen excitement that you can physically feel."

Lori leaned back in her chair. "You know, Carol says she thinks you're using the office to find a girlfriend."

Bill's face felt warm, and then he scowled. "I'm not using our office to pick up women. I normally don't date coworkers."

Lori answered, "I'm a little more than a coworker. I'm your employee. If we get caught fraternizing, we could both be fired. Maybe you can afford that to happen, Mr. Hot Shot Wall Street, but I came to this job directly from my MBA at Queens. If I lose my first job sleeping with my boss, my career is ruined before it's started."

Bill leaned forward, "Listen to me. I won't let it happen. Besides, I'm not the kind of boss to show favoritism to someone just because we're close."

Lori answered, "And I'm not the type of woman to go out on a date with her boss, but here we are."

Bill asked, "So, what are you saying?"

Lori responded, "I'm saying, let's slow down. If things look serious, we'll have some hard decisions to make."

Bill nodded silently.

His stomach cramped, and the restaurant disappeared.

He stood in his Condo in uptown, looking out over the city lights.

From behind, Lori's voice sounded like an angelic chorus in his ears, "This looks familiar."

Bill answered, "Let's hope the phone doesn't ring."

Lori's arms slipped around Bill's waist, and a shiver of pleasure and desire shot through his body.

Lori whispered in his ear, "Oh, is that a tremble of expectation?"

Bill giggled before he could stop himself. He felt Lori's fingers loosening his belt, and she blew in his ear.

Bill's body trembled again.

Lori took his hand and led him towards the bedroom. The door shut, and the room turned dark.

Something pressed against Bill's chest.

Lori paced around Bill's apartment, "I'm late. Do you know what that means?"

Bill answered sheepishly, "You're always late."

Lori picked up a pillow and threw it at him. "This isn't funny."

Bill smiled, "I think it's great news."

Lori stopped and waved her arms, "Great news! Are you crazy? Maybe I can end it without anyone finding out."

Bill leaped to his feet and wrapped his arms around her. "Don't you dare say that. I'd rather die first. That's our baby. Our family."

Lori wiggled loose from his embrace. "Don't you dare say that. I'm not some baby momma."

Bill shook his head, "That's not what I mean. Don't you see? I want to marry you."

Lori rolled her eyes, "Oh, so now you propose after you knock me up? That's some game."

Bill dropped to his knees, "Does this help?"

Lori crossed her arms, "Where's the ring, big boy. Don't have one, huh? Funny, you want to be a family so badly you didn't already have a ring before you got me pregnant."

Bill flopped down on the couch and exhaled in frustration. "I was planning on it. I just wasn't planning on you getting pregnant first."

Lori sat down next to him, "Well, that makes two of us. I told you we should take things slow."

Bill answered, "I thought we were, and we were careful."

Lori responded, "Not careful enough."

Bill grunted, and pain pierced his lower back. The apartment faded.

He now found himself on his knee at the beach. Tears trailed down Lori's cheeks, and she nodded vigorously. Then she faded from view. Light filled his vision and took the shape of a middle eastern man. His dark eyes glowed. Light surrounded his body, and any shadows disappeared.

The voice was warm, loving, comforting. "Bill, my child of many questions. Do you still doubt me?"

Bill gasped and could not stop his smile. Joy and peace filled his soul and the space around him.

The man continued, "I am the Father to the fatherless, a comforter and protector to those who are oppressed. My grace is from everlasting to everlasting."

Bill fell to the ground. He stammered, "Please, I'm sorry. I didn't know you were there."

The man's voice filled the air. "Didn't know? Who have you been speaking to? Who did you ask into your heart that night in the chapel?"

Bill pleaded, "I wasn't sure. It seemed like nothing changed. I didn't know what to think."

A hand lifted Bill's chin. The bearded man's eyes glowed with flames behind them. "Stand."

Bill stood.

The man continued, "I adopted you as my son. I paid for you with my blood. Would a father reject his son? Am I a man?"

Bill dove into his arms and his entire being seemed to vibrate. Bill stumbled back one step.

Two shadows appeared and then came into view. Bill gasped when he saw Lori and himself walking beside her.

Lori smiled and said, "It's okay, you can touch me."

Bill grabbed hold of her and buried his face in her hair and neck. She seemed younger and smelled like a field of flowers and a tropical paradise all at once.

Lori whispered in his ear, "You have to let go, honey. I have someone to show you."

Bill stepped back.

Lori pointed to the young man, "This is our son."

Bill's forehead crinkled, "I don't understand."

The man put out his hand, "I'm your son."

Bill stood there confused and then said, "But you were killed."

He and Lori nodded.

"Oh," said Bill. "What's your name?"

Lori answered, "His name is Tom."

Bill asked, "Why?"

"You'll understand one day. Come with us."

Bill held Lori's hand. The electricity between them was even more intense than he remembered. They strolled from the bright light onto an unfamiliar brown hill. Before the three of them stretched out the ocean. A terraced concrete patio came into view with an Infiniti pool looking out over the sea at its lowest point.

Lori said, "Watch."

A beautiful African American girl with thick flowing black hair came skipping out the back of the house and was making her way down to the pool. A tan little boy was floating on his back and splashing the water with his feet. The girl stopped in front of a man. Bill's mouth dropped open at the sight of himself.

The girl whispered, "Watch this, Daddy."

She pranced to the edge of the pool, hollered, "Cannonball," and landed next to the boy. The ensuing chaos left the boy coughing and the girl giggling.

Harold's voice sounded from behind them, "That's what you get, young man, for not paying attention."

Harold carried two beers and took one down Bill.

Bill said, "Lori, I don't want to see you do that to your cousin again. Coughing up water isn't fun."

Harold bumped Bill's shoulder, "You would know."

Lori whispered in his ear, "Time to go."

Bill said, "No, I don't understand."

Tom said, "You have a purpose."

Bill responded, "What? A pool party?"

Lori grabbed his face and turned him back to the scene. Darla and Carol came out the back door, and both looked very pregnant.

Carol hollered, "You boys planning on making us lunch? It's just like you two. All you want to do is sit around, drink beer, and keep the women knocked up."

Harold responded, "There are worse ways to live."

Darla answered, "Keep it up, funny man, and you'll be watching our kids while I take a six-month assignment in Russia."

Harold hollered, "Sorry," and he and Bill snickered.

Lori turned Bill's face back to her. "Don't you see, you have a family to raise. A future to build. God has a purpose for you and your family."

Bill looked deep into Lori's glistening black eyes, "But I love you. I can't raise a family with Carol."

Lori answered, "I'm dead, honey. We can't be together. I've moved on, and now you have to as well. Go and live the life God has given you."

A jolt of electricity hit his body, and he doubled over. Light filled his vision, and the warm, familiar voice rumbled, "All of my creation was made for my glory. The very rocks cry out my praise. Nothing you do is without my purpose. I am He who watches over the orphan and the fatherless. Go, be blessed, and bless others. Be forgiven and forgive others. Point those around you to my love and grace. As you have received, so give. Now, live."

Bill's whole body convulsed. His back hurt, his sides hurt, his chest hurt.

He could hear Carol, "Don't' you leave me."

Garcia pleaded, "You must live. Please don't die."

The light disappeared, and he could see shapes through his blurry eyes. Another massive cramp and water came pouring out of his mouth. Bill finally caught his breath and then expelled more of the putrid water until he was sure he would die anyway. A third wave hit, and by the fourth, Bill dry heaved and rolled over on the wet deck.

He wiped his eyes and blinked. Carol, Joshua, Harold, Garcia, and Maria hovered over him.

Joshua took a light and checked Bill's eyes. He said, "I wasn't sure you were coming back to us."

Bill sat up and answered, "I wasn't given a choice."

Carol's arms wrapped around Bill's shoulders, "Are you alright?"

He answered, "I am now."

Garcia said, "Okay, this is an evacuation. You'll take the Kodiak to the destroyer that's coming in closer from our right."

Harold looked up, "You can't let her sink."

Garcia answered, "Relax. We have another ship on its way to tow her back. Darla and Frank got the pumps working when you were saving your brother below. It can't keep the water out, but they should keep up once the ship is moving."

Harold argued, "I want to stay with the ship."

Garcia shook his head. "No doing. This is a CIA matter now. I have one dead fugitive in the hull and three more here, including Hunter."

Bill looked over and saw an old man with gray and red hair lying in his own blood and two others dead beside him.

Garcia continued, "You'll get it back when we're done with it. Trust me, you'll be glad we took it."

Harold said, "Fine, I'll stay with Bill."

Bill nodded, and Carol sat closer to him.

Garcia pointed to the ladder, "Alright, everyone on board. Bill, a doctor will check you out once you're on the ship. All of you will be taken back to the island. Stay there until we wrap things up and tell you it's safe."

Carol and Harold helped Bill to his feet. Harold half carried him to the Kodiak for the bumpy ride to the approaching ship.

CHAPTER 30

The white wooden rocker creaked under Bill. The large, covered porch brought back memories of the administrator's historic brick home in North Carolina. Joshua sat silently next to Bill, just like when he was a child. The two men stared blankly across the compound towards the empty bungalows. The sound of the ocean breeze and local birds was all that could be heard.

Bill reached over and took a drink from his sweet tea. The terror of his battle with Chuck just two days earlier seemed a distant memory. A heron flew across the Bungalow roofs and disappeared into the overgrowth behind the buildings.

Joshua said, "I've learned with Harold that dreams and visions are not always what they seem. You had a near-death experience, and the brain and spirit are still a mystery to science in many ways."

Bill looked over at the doctor. "According to Carol, I wasn't near death. I was dead."

Joshua nodded, "Yes, well, as I said, much of this is still a mystery. Your heart wasn't beating from a medical perspective, and you stopped breathing for a few minutes. However, some theories believe the body can go a certain amount of time in that condition and still revive, so there is some debate over when death actually happens."

Bill asked, "So, what? Are you saying my vision of God, Lori, and my son were tricks of my mind?"

Joshua answered, "I'm saying as a doctor I don't know."

Bill stared up into the clear blue sky and squinted. He asked, "What about not as a doctor?"

Joshua cleared his throat. "Well, as your brother in Christ, I would say God has given you a wonderful gift. There aren't too many people He reaches out to so directly, or allows to see loved ones after they have passed."

"So, you think I did see something?" asked Bill.

Joshua responded, "I think you're the only one who can answer that question. What does your spirit tell you? Down in your gut, what do you think?"

Bill looked down at the ground, and his lips curled up. He answered, "God said I was his child of many questions. I guess even when I get the answers, I have a hard time accepting them without more questions."

Joshua said, "Well, I suppose you have to ask yourself this question. Are your questions more important than the answers you were given?"

Bill sat back and stared into Joshua's peaceful eyes. He answered, "That's a good question."

The two men sat quietly and slowly finished their drinks. Bill heard a door close on his left and saw Carol coming down from her bungalow next to his. She had on a yellow bikini with a white wrap. Bill could not take his eyes off her until she was standing in front of him.

Carol smiled and said, "You know, you can blink now."

Bill's eyes fluttered, and his face felt flush. "Sorry, I was thinking about something."

"Obviously," responded Carol.

Joshua asked, "Are you headed to the pool?"

Carol nodded, "I'm going to live the good life and hang out with the girls. You boys aren't invited."

Joshua answered, "This sounds like trouble."

Carol started to walk towards the main house, looked over her shoulder, and said, "I'll let Maria know you said that."

Joshua looked over at Bill and quietly said, "Now I am in trouble."

Bill laughed and stood up. "If you'll excuse me, I think I'd like to go for a walk alone. I want to hide before your wife shows up."

Joshua looked up. "Coward."

"You know it."

The two men laughed as Bill headed towards the familiar trail he had found when he first came to the island. There was a peacefulness to the place now that the Franks had left. Maria made sure food was available, and it was everyone for themselves when it came to cleaning. Harold promised staff would arrive in a couple of days to handle the maintenance.

Bill made his way down the path towards the beach. He stopped halfway and listened. There were no sounds of footsteps, an engine starting up, wheels on the crushed shelled road, or distant voice on the breeze. A momentary change in the wind direction brought the sound of women laughing, and Bill wondered if Carol was joking about Joshua and him. Rustling in the bushes nearby made Bill jump, and he continued his journey at a brisk pace.

He arrived at the empty beach and looked at Harold's favorite rock. Climbing up on top, he noticed the great view of the clear water. Small barracuda, blackjack, and others swam in the shallows to avoid larger predators. A short distance out, dark grasses covered the deeper bottom, and Bill wondered if he would be fortunate enough to see a manatee.

He was tempted for a moment to wade into the shallows. Then scowled and pull his knees up to his chest.

Bill looked up towards the sky and said, "I don't know what to think. Everything I have asked you answered. Or at least it seems like you did. Did you really let me see Lori and my son? Am I going to have a family with Carol?"

"What about me?" Harold's voice caused Bill to release his knees and almost fall off the rock.

"When did you walk up?"

Harold continued his way over to Bill, "When you started praying."

Bill's forehead furrowed, "I wanted to be alone."

Harold slapped Bill on the back, "Yea, that's what Doc said. I figured I'd find you here. I need a fishing buddy."

Bill answered, "Some other time. I have some things to think about."

"Some of my best thinking has been done on that fishing boat. Well, maybe not my best thinking."

"What does that mean?" asked Bill.

"It's a long story. Look, you and Doc like to sit around and think alone too much. Sometimes it helps to bounce your thoughts of someone you can trust. You can't trust anyone more than your own brother, especially after I saved your life."

Bill nodded, "Where are the poles?"

"On the boat."

Bill started to slip off the rock but stopped and scowled, "I don't know. I've had enough of boats and water for a lifetime, thanks."

Harold shook his head, "Oh, no, you haven't. My dad taught me a valuable lesson when I was a kid. He used to take me camping out in the Mojave. We would hike, have campfires, the whole bit. Anyway, when I was big enough, he taught me to ride a motorcycle. The first day I soloed, I crashed and bruised my shin. I wanted nothing to do with that motorbike.

"Dad told me that if a horse throws you off, you have to get back on, or you'll be afraid of horses the rest of your life. I didn't understand what he meant at first. He said allowing external things to control me would cause me to live in fear and never reach my potential."

Bill answered, "So, you're saying that me wanting to avoid the water and boats two days after I was almost killed could ruin the rest of my life?"

Harold smiled, "Exactly. Now, come on, let's see if we can catch something worth eating."

Bill hung his legs over the rock, "I suppose if I keep saying no, you're going to bug me until I relent."

"Yep. Maybe, I'll just carry you and toss you onboard."

Bill sighed, slipped off the rock, and followed Harold off the beach.

CHAPTER 31

The cabin cruiser sat silently in the still waters. Small desert keys could be seen in every direction. Harold brought a thermos full of rum runner that he claimed was Garcia's recipe, so there were no concerns about navigating later. They had managed to catch some modest groupers, but nothing either man felt was worth taking back to eat.

Harold asked, "So, this isn't so bad, right?"

Bill shrugged, "I'd call it peaceful."

"Good. Now, I have a question for you. Well, it's more of a proposal."

Bill stopped staring blankly at the horizon and turned towards his brother. "What sort of proposal?"

"Well, my understanding is that you're between jobs. I have some offshore funds my parents' set up for me in case of an emergency."

Bill raised an eyebrow, "What kind of emergency?"

Harold shrugged, "Well, I guess a government take-over or something that would put my future at a high risk."

Bill sat up, "Wait, isn't that what happened to you? I mean, your company almost collapsed, and it looks like you were in pretty deep with the CIA."

Harold nodded, "I was able to avoid using the money. I couldn't bring myself to cut and run and leave all those workers and their family's stranded."

"And if it happens again?"

Harold answered, "I like to think I've learned a few things. One of those things is that there are circumstances I won't always be able to control. Next time there may not be a Garcia or Alice looking out for me. Not to mention, I have a wife now, and hopefully, one day, some kids. I'll need to put them first."

Bill reached for the thermos and started to pour a drink. "So, what do you want from me?"

"I need someone I can trust to handle those accounts. How would you like to manage them?"

Bill asked, "What sort of fees will I be paid."

"Well if you are half as good as Carol told me, you'll be doing well."

Bill took a sip from his cup and then asked, "What does that mean?"

"I'm going to pay you Wall Street's standard rates plus commission based on the funds' year-end performance."

Bill nodded. "Okay, I suppose this is a silly question, but how much is in there now?"

Harold looked Bill in the eye, "As of this morning, one hundred and fifty million."

Bill's eyes widened, "Most people would put at least some of that into a charity fund instead of hiding it offshore."

Harold nodded. "Well, most people don't make nukes. I want to grow that big enough to not only look after my own interest but my employees. I never want to be in a position again where somebody can force me to do things I disagree with."

"Even your country?"

Harold answered, "Especially my country."

Bill put down his cup. "That's a tempting offer."

Harold continued, "I'm not done.

"I want you to help me diversify Parabolic Defense Systems. I lost a lot of good people when the CIA focused our company on conventional arms, and for good reasons. Causing death and destruction shouldn't be the only thing we're about. I'd like to see us get more involved in the new private space race."

Bill asked, "You want to compete against SpaceX?"

"No. I want to find a way to partner with them, and Blue Origin, and others. We have some great rocket scientists with more experience than the whiz kids working at these new companies. I think we can bring some value to their table. You'd handle the money side of any partnerships we manage to put together."

"Is that a commission or salary position?"

Harold responded, "That part of the job is salary since that job is part of PDS."

Bill finished his drink and then asked, "Are there any contingencies?"

"Doc and I were talking yesterday while you were resting. Maria wants to go back to North Carolina and work with the orphans one or two days a week as a volunteer. Doc used to have a very lucrative online counseling blog before we had to go into hiding. He wants to bring that back. Since it's online, he's flexible about where he lives.

"Adam called Joshua and said there is a rumor going around that a pandemic may be coming. Personally, I think it's just the media. Still, Doc says Adam has it on good authority from some medical physicians he knows. Anyway, Adam wants Joshua to come to North Carolina and teach psychologists and psychiatrists how to do remote counseling through the internet. Evidently, they're expecting folks to get locked down. I hope the rumors are wrong, but who knows."

Bill asked, "What does that have to do with me?"

"Doc and I talked with Carol yesterday. She tells us your house in the suburbs around Charlotte is pretty nice."

Bill said, "Well, nice is relative. Compared to a lot of the homes, it's pretty modest."

Harold stood, stretched his back, and looked back over at Bill. "Well, by west coast standards, it's upper middle income. Anyway, Doc is interested in swapping his house for yours if you're interested. I'll pay for the movers so we can get the ball rolling ASAP. Doc says Adam claims we only have a few weeks or maybe a couple of months before things go sideways."

Bill thought about his vision while he stared at his fishing rod.

After a couple of minutes, Harold asked, "Are you still with me?"

Bill blinked a couple of times and found Harold sitting next to him. "Yea, sorry. I was just pondering your offer. I've never even seen Joshua's house."

Harold answered, "Carol warned us you'd say that. As soon as Garcia arrives with the all-clear, we're flying back to Malibu. I want you to join us. Joshua and Maria will show you around."

"I'm not sure Carol can go on such short notice. I'm sure her family is worried about her."

Harold asked, "Why would Carol come? Did you pop the question without telling anyone?"

Bill coughed and took a breath. "No, I mean, well, it's hard to explain."

"Hard to explain? Now you have me curious, bro. What's so hard to explain?"

Bill sat back and looked Harold in the eye. "When I was dead, I saw God. He spoke to me and showed me things."

"That's awesome."

Bill asked, "That doesn't freak you out?"

"Freak me out?" Harold started to laugh and then said, "Bro, I've seen ghosts and a demon."

Bill's eyes widened, "Are you serious."

"Yes. I was dealing with a lot of hate. I hated John for causing my parents' death, and I hated myself for killing. I was starting down a dark road. I had to learn to truly forgive my enemies. I didn't think that was possible given our little issue with striking out at those who hurt us.

"I learned a couple of lessons along the way. First, God created me this way, and if it wasn't for my strength and anger, more good people would have been hurt or killed. Second, I don't have all the answers. Growing up around rocket scientists and engineers, not to mention Joshua, makes it seem like there's an answer to every problem, but there isn't. A universe is a vast place, and God created all sorts of amazing things, both on earth and beyond what we usually see day to day. It's alright if I don't know everything that's going on. I don't need to know unless I'm involved in it at some point.

"So, tell me, Bro. What did God show you?"

Bill answered, "Well, he showed us. I was married to Carol, and we were dads and living at this big house overlooking the ocean."

Harold held up his hand, "Stop there. That's meant for you, not me. So, I see your problem, I think. I offer you this position in California. Obviously, that's where that vision was. I know because that's my house. Now you're worried if you don't take the job and marry Carol, you'll mess stuff up."

Bill nodded. "I spent most of my life asking God to prove he existed. In a moment, God helped me understand that he'd always been there. When I saw God, he let me see Lori and our son, who was killed. They were so beautiful and happy. They were far more satisfied in heaven than they ever would have been down here. I understand now that God's view of our lives is different than ours. It's like you said, we can't have all the answers.

"But now I'm worried I'll screw up God's plans. What if Carol says no to my proposal? Worse, what if I'm marrying her because of the vision?"

Harold slapped Bill's back, "Bro, you think too much. We're talking about God here, and you can't mess up his plans. He controls the universe and beyond. I have an idea. Why don't you go back home? Take some time to unwind because you've been through a lot. Believe me, I'm planning on soaking up some of the California sun when I get back.

"Spend some time with Carol. I'll be honest, I've seen how you two look at each other. You're not just friends, at least not now. Darla told me the first day she saw you two that you would end up together, and she isn't wrong about people."

Bill nodded, "Women's intuition."

"CIA. Look, give me a call when you feel like your head's clear. If you're interested, I'll fly you out to see the place, no pressure. The offer stands on Joshua's house whether you decide to remain single or get married. If you tell me no, I'd love to have you visit my estate as my brother, and we'll go act like tourists around Southern California."

Bill smiled and nodded, "That sounds perfect. I waited my whole life for a family. I think finally meeting you has made some of it worth it."

Harold laughed, "Some of it?"

He reached over and gave Bill a bear hug, and Bill returned the favor. Harold's fishing pole suddenly bent towards the water. He jumped to get his rod, and Bill went to the bridge and started the motor. The two brothers fought the fish for several minutes.

Harold yelled, "Bro, I see it, grab the net."

Bill cut the engine and left the bridge, and grabbed the large fishing net. Harold made his way to the rear of the boat to the dive platform. His eyes widened.

Harold yelled, "Cut the line."

Bill stared intently into the water. The shadow of an eight-foot bull shark swam this way and that. The rear of the boat drifted in the direction of the fish. Bill turned and ran for the cabin. He quickly dug through the toolbox and found the tool he needed.

He returned to Harold, extended his hand, and said, "Here, kill it."

Harold looked at him wide-eyed, "Are you crazy? That's just a large wrench."

Bill smiled, "Put your strength behind it."

Harold shook his head, "I hate sharks."

Bill pushed the wrench against Harold's chest, "Sounds like there's a horse you need to climb back up on."

Harold took the wrench, and Bill grabbed the pole. The shark nearly pulled him over until Bill quickly regained his footing.

Harold turned to Bill from the back of the boat and growled, "Not funny, bro."

Bill replied, "Kill it."

Bill fought the reel and pulled the shark closer to the dive deck, and the small cabin cruiser drifted towards the shark. The fish saw Harold at the water line and swam towards him. Harold raised the wrench over his head. He roared as it came down, and the whole boat shuddered. The fish stopped moving and drifted near the surface.

Bill started to help Harold when his brother grabbed it by the gills and tossed it onto the deck.

Bill said, "Great job."

Harold scowled, but then his lips curled up, and his entire face lit up. "That felt good."

Bill responded, "Looks like you were right about getting back up on the horse. Why don't I bring my line in, and we'll head back to the island."

Harold nodded, stepped over the fish, dropped the wrench in the toolbox, and started the engine.

CHAPTER 32

Carol's fingernails gently flowed down Bill's t-shirt. The skin on his back tingled and then relaxed. The air was mild, the breeze lightly kissed his cheeks. The solitary iron and wood bench contoured around his hips. Everything at that moment felt perfect.

Carol stopped. Bill closed his eyes and whispered, "Please, don't stop."

Carol took a single finger and traced random patterns around Bill's back, and the soreness of his battle with Chuck, the tension and stress of his loss, and the fear of the unknown all disappeared. At that moment, Bill did not care what would happen five minutes from now. If he had his way, the two of them would remain like this forever.

Carol stopped, and Bill let out a sigh.

Carol said, "I'm sorry, my arms can only take so much."

Bill sat up and gave her a hug. Carol's dark, silky neck felt good against his cheek. He gave it a gentle kiss and then sat back and said, "I appreciate it. You helped me relax."

Carol looked into his eyes and asked, "So, what are you going to do?"

"I'm going back to North Carolina with you."

Carol's brow wrinkled, "I love you, but you need to get your head on straight."

Bill looked at Carol, the water, the sky, and his mouth dropped open. He stood, walked to the water's edge, turned, and said, "I don't understand."

Carol looked up at him, "Harold gave you an amazing offer. You can work with your brother. The two of you can get to know each other. Not to mention you have a sister-in-law. You're crazy if you think I'm going to be the cause of you leaving what you've wanted your whole life."

Bill sat down hard on the bench, and the iron reverberated. "What I wanted my whole life is a family, my family."

Carol grabbed a fist full of his t-shirt, "Listen to me, baby. You have a family. Maybe you should get to know them before you start your own."

Bill reached up and held her hand against his chest, "But what if I lose you?"

Carol rolled her eyes, "How many times do I have to tell you I'll be here. I know you love me, and you should know how I'm feeling about you."

Carol released her hand, and Bill stood up and walked to the water's edge. Just below its surface, several manatees floated, almost unseen in the reflection of the sun. Bill watched them and wondered if they were looking for Harold.

He turned to face Carol. "You know, Harold is planning on keeping the island."

Carol shrugged, "So, he's a one-percenter. That's what they do."

Bill shook his head, "No. He's planning on using it as a getaway for his employees."

Carol scowled, "What does that have to do with anything?"

Bill walked over, kissed her forehead, and sat down. "Don't' you see, he's moving back to his childhood home and keeping the island. He's doing both."

Carol answered, "I'm not getting you."

"I don't have to choose to live in California or North Carolina. I can spend time in both places. I can get to know my family, we can spend time getting to know each other, and I can get to know your family."

Carol's tone turned somber, "Uh oh, I forgot about that."

Bill asked, "Forgot about what?"

"Let's just say not everyone in my family is as progressive as we are." Answered Carol.

Bill shrugged, "That's their problem."

Carol leaned in and gave him a short, soft kiss, and sat back up. "I hope you still think that way after you meet them."

"Is it going to cause a problem. You know, like break up your family? I would rather lose you than have that happen."

Carol grabbed his face and thrust her lips against his. Her long, deep kiss left him lightheaded. She let go, and he grabbed the back of the bench to steady himself.

Carol's eyes danced as she looked at him, "Nobody is going to come between us."

Bill nodded, slack-jawed.

A rustling in the bush caught their attention. Bill turned to find Harold down the beach near the trail, shaking a branch.

Harold cleared his throat, "Sorry, I didn't want to startle you. Garcia and Darla are landing soon. They want us to wait at the house if you don't mind."

Carol answered, "Why should we mind? I hope I can finally get back home. My momma has threatened to turn my cats loose in the streets if I don't get my tail home soon."

Bill asked, "Oh, they let you call your mom?"

Carol nodded.

Harold waived, "I'll see you in a few minutes," and he left.

Carol and Bill stood, held hands, and began their slow walk down the beach and the trail.

"So, what's your dad like?"

Carol answered, "He's very protective."

"So am I. We should get along great."

Carol stayed silent as they made their way through the front door and found Joshua and Maria sitting at the bar with their rum runners.

Joshua raised his glass, "Come, join us for the celebration."

Bill asked for beer for him and Carol.

Joshua said, "I thought you were starting to like our little punches? I make sure they're healthy and easy on the liver."

Carol answered, "I'm not an island girl. Give me a fifteen-year-old scotch neat and a good book to read by the fire."

Bill shrugged, "I like everything, but I'm in the mood to get back home, and this beer takes me there."

Maria spoke up, "I miss North Carolina too. The small orphans need me, and Joshua's hometown reminds me of my village in Mexico where I lived when I was a little girl."

Bill responded, "Yea, we'll have to talk about that later. After I've had a few weeks to think about it."

Joshua reached out and took Carol and Bill by the shoulders, "You two have been through a lot. You should take time to recover and think through your lives alone and together. We all need to do the same. Maria has not seen her home in California for some time. To be honest, we never thought we'd get to go back."

Carol said, "Who knows, you may decide to never leave again."

Maria shook her head. "The orphans need me. The Bible commands we should care for them. I would never put my comfort ahead of such wonderful children."

Carol left Bill's side and took the seat next to Maria. "I like you. Tell me more about growing up in Mexico."

Joshua nodded his head at Bill, "I think this is our cue to let the women talk. Let's grab a couple of lounge chairs.

The two men left Maria to tell her story to Carol, and they picked out two comfortable chairs facing the sun. They each took a sip of their drink, sighed, and closed their eyes.

Joshua said, "This place has a different vibe when there isn't someone out there looking to kill you."

"Yea, I actually feel relaxed."

The sound of tires crunching and sliding on the seashell lane outside the house brought both men to attention.

Joshua said, "Well, it's time to find out if we've been permanently released."

CHAPTER 33

Bill followed as Harold led the procession straight to the bar. Darla was dressed in a navy-blue pants suit. Garcia looked uncharacteristically dressed up, but his trademark sunglasses were still in place. Harold left Bill to join his wife. Darla and Harold whispered at the end of the bar, and Harold's hands kept fluttering about as he spoke.

Joshua said, "This isn't the mood I expected from these two. I wonder if it's bad news."

Garcia raised his voice, "Everyone, let's get together at that table."

Darla and Harold stopped their conversation. Carol and Maria grabbed their drinks and walked over together. Bill noticed Maria had gotten Carol to try a rum runner. Everyone sat down, except for Darla and Garcia, who stood at the head of the table.

Darla spoke up, "First, let me give everyone the good news. We're officially free."

Applause broke out, and Joshua pumped his fist in the air.

Darla put up her hands to quiet the group and then continued. "There are some complications that Garcia will address, but let me finish with the good news. All of us will be able to return to our homes. For Joshua, Maria, Harold, and myself, that means we are going home to Malibu. Bill, you and Carol will be returned to Charlotte."

Joshua spoke up, "What about you, agent Garcia?"

Darla stood silent, looking at her partner. Garcia responded, "That's classified."

Harold rolled his eyes, "We should've known."

Carol asked, "So, what's the bad news?"

Everyone sat quietly. Darla walked over and took an empty seat next to her husband, and took his hand.

Garcia removed his glasses and cleared his throat. "I'm not sure how to say this. A pandemic is coming."

Bill interrupted, "Come on, there's a pandemic rumor three or four times a year in the markets. They never turn out to be true."

Bill looked around the table and noticed Harold looking straight at him, slowly shaking his head.

Garcia continued, "I wish it was a rumor. Our people in China confirmed some sort of biological agent was accidentally released from a lab in Wuhan. How contagious and deadly it is, we don't know. I've heard all kinds of rumors. We've been made aware of at least two planes that have come to the U.S. from Wuhan since the virus was discovered. Whether the Chinese government was aware of the situation before then we don't know, and the communist government there isn't sharing.

"The President briefed us while we were in Washington of a likely government shutdown."

Bill interrupted, "You mean like Washington D.C. or the whole country?"

Garcia leaned forward against the chair in front of him. "The entire country."

Bill responded, "That's insane."

Garcia stood back up. "It may not be as crazy as you think. China's leaders have shared they are heading that way, and our allies are planning to follow the same path if it appears in their country."

Carol spoke up, "So, what you're saying is everyone here is exchanging a tropical prison for house arrest."

Garcia answered, "I'm afraid so."

Carol asked, "How long?"

Garcia said, "We don't know."

Darla stood back up and walked next to Garcia, "There is a small silver lining for the people at this table."

Bill said, "I can't wait to hear this."

Darla ignored his quip. "Obviously, we haven't been near any of this. As long as we remain isolated, we can move around more freely. The government is coming up with a protocol to identify the virus. Once they do, we can all be tested as needed if we want to do any traveling.

"Harold and I are going to volunteer the PDS jet to anyone who needs to come to California or would like to return to the island if things get worse."

Harold asked, "What about my yacht?"

Garcia frowned, "What about it?"

Harold said, "Well, I want to know when I'm getting it back, and can we use it to travel?"

Garcia answered, "What I am about to tell you can't leave this table. Carol, Bill, normally I would make you leave, but I want you to know your part of this family. That said, nothing can be shared with anyone else, especially to family members."

Bill answered, "I don't have any other family."

Carol said, "He's talking to me. I know when to keep my mouth shut."

Garcia nodded. "Harold, your yacht is being looked over with a fine-tooth comb. We want to figure out what sort of explosives were used to breach the hull and where they came from.

"In the meantime, we were able to find and capture the small sub Hunter was using. Thanks to our cold war hydrophones, the craft was easy to pick up when the crew panicked and headed for deeper water after our ships began to patrol the surrounding area. It didn't take us too long to track it down. Because of the intel we found on the vessel, we were able to fire two cruise missiles at a camp near the southern border of Turkmenistan."

Joshua said, "I thought Chuck said their compound is in the center of Iran."

Garcia nodded, "It is, but the sub had intel on an ISIS training camp that Hunter supplied with arms. Satellite images confirm over fifty people were killed, and the camp was wiped out. Assets on the ground confirmed it was an ISIS training camp. We were able to remove some mid-level leadership in the attack."

Harold asked, "What about Iran?"

Darla shook her head, "If we launch anything into Iran, it will start a war, possibly a global war."

Carol sat back and crossed her arms, "So, Hunter's little racist camp of super-warriors is safe and sound."

Garcia frowned, "I wouldn't call them safe. We've spoken to Iran through side channels. That village is a liability for them. We hope they'll encourage them to leave. Since Hunter is dead, and Harold was the heir apparent, they have no chosen leader. With any luck, they'll break up and try to find their way back to where they all came from."

Bill said, "The "cut off the head" theory."

Garcia and Darla nodded. Carol asked, "And how has that worked for you in the past?"

Darla looked at Garcia and then answered, "We'll cross that bridge if we come to it."

Joshua spoke up, "Well, none of this is our problem anyway, right?"

Darla answered, "Exactly. None of the remaining people have any reason to come after any of you. The submarine was captured by the navy ship, and Hunter was killed by the CIA. None of you are involved."

Harold spoke up, "Can we get back to my ship?"

Darla answered, "Of course, dear. Garcia was trying to tell you that the CIA will have to keep it for a while for more intel. In return, they are paying to have all the repairs completed. That's quite an offer since it looks like it could run into the seven figures. I'm not sure I'd let you spend that kind of money."

Harold crossed his arms, "Fine. So, if we are still locked down when I get it back, I can get out on the open ocean and away from whatever insanity is going on in the country."

Garcia answered, "I don't think you'll want to use it. My intel tells me of at least two cruise ships with signs of this new virus. It's only a couple of people, and they are keeping it very quiet. Still, their ports of destination have already refused them docking. It's just a matter of time before the papers get hold of this. After that, I would be surprised if any ships will be allowed anywhere.

"Once things get that bad, I can give you access to military airstrips, and of course, you have your own here. Those are your best bets for travel."

Maria asked, "When can we leave?"

Darla said, "Anytime you like."

"I want to go home today."

Joshua gently touched his wife's shoulder. "Easy, sweetheart. We need time to pack."

Carol said, "I want to leave today, too."

Darla nodded, "Okay, so you and Bill are going today?"

Bill shook his head, "No, I'm staying. I want to spend a day or two getting to know you and my brother if that's alright."

Harold slapped the table, "Alright? That's a terrific idea."

Bill looked at Carol, "I promise to call as soon as I arrive home."

Garcia nodded, "Terrific. Carol, I'll fly with you as far as Charlotte. I have a company plane that's going to take me to my destination."

Harold asked, "So, just like that, it's over?"

Darla nodded, "Just like that."

Harold's eyes glistened.

Joshua asked, "What's wrong?"

Harold choked back his tears. "When we started this journey, I had a mom and dad, and of course you Doc, and Maria. I can't forget my best friend, Tom. Now I have my brother back and new friends I would trust with my life. I just never thought this is where my life would end up."

Bill answered, "Yea. I lost the one family before we even got started, and now I have another."

Joshua said, "God's ways are truly mysterious. Through our pain and loss, new beginnings emerge."

Garcia added, "Death and resurrection, it's all around us."

Carol looked at Garcia and Joshua, "You two now preacher men?"

Garcia smiled.

Joshua answered, "No, just a believer who has learned more over the last few months than I thought I knew my entire life."

Carol added, "I guess that's worth more than blowing up some camp in the middle of nowhere."

Bill took her hand and kissed the back of it. "I agree."

EPILOGUE

Bill sat in his family room. The sunroom door sat open, and the winter sun shone just below the tall trees at noon and provided soft warmth to the tinted glass panels. Bill stared at Ezekiel three on his laptop. He ran his hand through his black, wavy hair.

Bill looked up at the cathedral ceiling, "Okay, so you have made me this way. I've sat here longer than seven days, and I'm not even bitter like Ezekiel. What am I supposed to do?"

He closed his computer's lid, got up, and headed to the kitchen for more coffee. The Keurig rumbled and hissed with the promise of more caffeine. Bill grabbed his full mug and walked out into the backyard. The crisp, Carolina air met his face. He put his cup down on the glass table and stuffed his hands into the front pockets of his jeans.

A red cardinal and his mate danced and fluttered for position on the bird feeder. The small pond bubbled and cold water trickled from its small waterfalls. Two squirrels attempted to hide in the bushes and carefully watched Bill's next move. Unnoticed, Bill watched the couple next door sip their coffee and enjoy the cold morning huddled together talking on their deck. A sense of loneliness settled over his heart.

The noise of his front gate being jerked open caught his attention. Carol stood there in a fleece jacket that sat on top of the hidden layer of clothes beneath. Skinny jeans and Nikes completed her outfit. Carol's thick, curly black hair hung loose, covering much of her face from the dry, cold air. Bill felt his face warm against the cold air and waved her in his direction.

She asked, "I guess you don't get much company?"

Bill cocked his head.

Carol continued, "I rang your doorbell three times. Isn't it a little cold to be hiding from the world back here?"

Bill nodded and grabbed his coffee, "Come on in, the sunroom is warmer."

The two entered the glass room. Carol joined him on an old glider he'd picked up at an estate sale. Bill put his coffee down on the end table and faced Carol.

"I'm not really hiding. I've been spending a lot of time rereading my Bible and thinking about everything that's happened. Ezekiel and I have spent a lot of time together. I can relate to his life. Everyone thinks about Ezekiel because the first part of the book sounds like a UFO encounter.

"Did you know that Ezekiel said God talked to him and then physically moved him through the air and placed him in another location?"

Carol nodded.

Bill continued, "It says he was bitter and even tried to get loose. God spoke to Ezekiel and told him everything he had to do, and Ezekiel didn't want any part of it. Even after he was placed with the exiles to be a prophet, Ezekiel just sat there for a week. Essentially, God had to threaten him to make him do what he was supposed to do."

Carol asked, "So, you're hanging out at home until God threatens you?"

Bill shook his head. "That isn't what I'm saying. I just want to make sure I'm hearing God's voice."

Carol reached over and took Bill's hand. Her cold fingers brought shivers up Bill's arms. Her dark eyes glistened and danced as she stared into his. "Look, you told me you saw Jesus. He spoke to you. You won't tell me what you saw, but I know you said you felt peace and love. Baby, we're his children, adopted through Christ's blood. You should be able to understand that."

Bill answered, "Of course."

Carol continued, "Okay, then unless he called you to go be a missionary in India and you're refusing, you should move forward with your life."

Bill pulled her hands to his lips. Her cold, smooth skin felt good against his lips, and he held them against his cold, dry lips for several seconds before letting her go. "I guess I'm afraid. The last woman I loved was taken from me. What if this is some sort of test?"

Carol stood and looked out at the birds crowding a nearby feeder. "Then I'll go join Lori and your son. From what you said, it's better there."

Bill stood up next to her, "I'm not sure I can take that again."

Carol turned to Bill, "Unless God showed you that I'm dying, you're worrying about things that will never happen the way you are playing them out."

Bill slipped his arm around her, "Then maybe I should make a move."

Carol turned to Bill. The sun, the room, everything evaporated as her lips met his. His very soul felt the same joy and peace he had experienced in death. His hand started to slide down her back when she grabbed his arm, pulled it away, and stepped back.

Bill's jaw went slack, and he started to stammer.

Carol raised her hand, "Slow down there, baby. You don't get past these lips until you put a ring on this finger."

Bill back peddled until his back pressed against the glass wall. "I, I don't understand. I thought we felt the same way about each other. You know I'd give my life for you."

Carol smiled and slowly walked towards Bill. He could feel a thrill run up his spine and her fingertips caused his cheek to tingle. Her voice was soft, smooth, quiet. "Baby, you don't win a woman, at least not this woman. Love isn't earned. Love simply exists, and the ultimate love is the commitment, not the bedroom.

"I don't want to be conquered or won. That's what you do for a prize or property. I want to be loved, living freely together, choosing daily to stay together through the good and the bad."

Carol took a step back, and Bill rubbed his forehead. "I thought you loved me because you know I'd do any-thing for you."

Carol kissed Bill's forehead and sauntered back to the glider. "Silly man, I think Maria is right. Boys are stupid. I'm not here because you'll do anything for me. I'm here because I want to be here. You're a good man, somebody I can trust. I can see us gray, wrinkled, and smiling while grandkids run around the house.

"I thought you wanted to be with me for the same reasons."

Bill rushed over, sat next to Carol, and held her hands. He clung to them for fear he might not feel them again. "I do. I mean, I want to spend my life with you too. I just thought I had to convince you. My whole life has been about working, fighting, scratching for everything. Education, money, friends, even my first family."

Carol looked compassionately into his eyes and then kissed his cheek for several seconds before sitting back.

She responded, "My poor, dear. It's no wonder your faith faded. You don't have to fight for me. Just be here."

Bill asked, "How do I do that?"

A smile spread across Carol's face, "I'll show you how."

Bill asked, "You mean after we're married."

Carol laughed, and Bill's felt his face flush. She said, "No, this has to happen before we're married. Then, when we're ready, you'll face Daddy. I won't marry anyone without his blessing."

Bill said, "You make it sound like he's worse than facing Chuck."

Carol stood and looked down at Bill, "You'll be ready when the time comes. Hey, do you have anything to eat around here?"

Bill answered, "Let's go to Mac's for some BBQ."

Carol nodded, "That sounds good. From the rumbling in the media, we may not have many days left to go out."

Bill stood, "Yea, what's going to happen if things are shut down? I mean, how will we see each other?"

Carol answered, "Isn't that the advantage of having powerful friends? Besides, it's nobody's business if we see each other. We'll just need to avoid the public because of the pandemic, like Garcia said."

Bill pointed to the opened door leading into the house, "Well, let's grab some food while we still can."

***

The smell of sea salt filled his nostrils. Bill played in the sand with his toes and let the sun warm his face. Carol sat on her beach towel, stacking a pile of sand in the center of Bill's stomach.

Bill commented, "You know, that's a really slow way to bury someone in the sand."

"I'm trying to decide how much of you I want to bury."

Bill shaded his eyes with his arm and looked up at her. "What do you mean?"

"You're leaving me."

Bill sat up and the sand tumbled onto their towels. He ignored the gritty dirt working its way into his bathing suit as he turned to face her. He reached for her hands and held this tight. "I am not."

Carol cocked her head, "I thought you're moving to California."

Bill sighed, let go of her hands, looked at the sky, and then back to Carol. He sighed again. "I don't understand. I mean, I thought we were going to California."

Carol held up her graceful dark hand, "Do you see a ring anywhere?"

Bill leaned in to kiss her fingers and she pulled her hand away. He crossed his arms and looked down. "You said I had to ask your dad's permission before I could even think about giving you an engagement ring."

Carol nodded, "That's true. So, you shouldn't assume I'm going to be leaving all my family and friends for you before I say I do."

Bill stood up, "I need to go for a walk."

"May I join you?"

Bill extended his hand; Carol took it and the two strolled along the beach together. The warm water washed over their ankles and across their feet. They held hands and strolled towards the Ocean Isle pier.

Suddenly, Carol let go of him and dove her hands under the water. She came up with a fresh sand dollar. She handed it to Bill. "Here, to remember our trip. Be careful, it's fragile."

Bill took it and the two continued walking. He stopped after another ten yards. "Is this a game to you?"

Carol's mouth dropped open. "A game? Why would you say that?"

Bill pointed back from where they came. "Oh, I don't know. Over there you made it sound like we could break up, and then you hand me this sand dollar to remember the trip like it's rainbows and lollipops. I can't tell if you love me or if you're toying with me."

Carol wrapped her arms around him. She whispered in his ear. "I'm doing a little of both."

Carol stepped back and Bill cleared his throat. "When you say it like that, it takes on a whole other meaning. But, you have to understand, I didn't grow up like other guys. I haven't really dated, at least not until college, and even then, it was never serious. Of course, Lori and I were serious, but that was different. You've taught me so much about men and women and healthy relationships, but I still feel lost sometimes. You know, like I'm going to fail you, us, this whole thing."

Carol gently pushed her fingernail into his chin and guided his face so they were looking into one another's eyes. Bill swallowed at the dancing dark eyes that seem to look deep into his soul.

Carol said, "This isn't a test. The only way to fail is to stop trying. Love isn't about making mistakes and losing. The only way to lose at love is to give up when you do make a mistake. We'll both succeed and fail together. When we do fail, we'll forgive each other and move forward together."

Bill nodded and then pointed over his shoulder, "Let's head back to the hotel."

***

The two sat on the wooden deck of Bill's hotel room. Their legs were propped up on the railing and the two of them slowly sipped their drinks. Bill watched a brother and sister burying their father in the sand. He pointed between the posts, "You see, that's how you bury somebody."

"To be fair, there are two of them, and they are much younger than I am."

Bill laughed, "True."

"What? Are you calling me old?"

Beer shot out of Bill's nose and he choked and laughed. Once he had gotten his air back he replied, "No, you're just not a little girl."

Carol smiled but said nothing in return.

Bill's eyelids began to feel heavy when Carol poked his shoulder and asked, "What are you going to do when the bigots come?"

Bill rubbed his face, dropped his feet on the deck and turned towards Carol. "Come again."

"You know, the bigots, racists, whatever you want to call them. You know they'll try and cause trouble. A black woman and a white man, there'll be problems."

Bill grabbed her hand, "Why didn't you bring this up before? I mean, if it scares you, I don't want to force you into something that could hurt you."

"That's not what I mean. I've lived with it my whole life. I want to know what you are going to do. I can tell you, both black and white people won't like what we're doing. Are you able to handle it?"

Bill laughed, "I think you've seen what I can handle."

Carol pulled back her hand. "That's my point. I don't want you in jail, or worse for attacking someone. Are you going to be able to walk away?"

Bill sat silent. He had only recently learned who he really was inside. Could he keep the beast from showing itself if the love of his life was threatened?

Bill answered honestly, "I don't know. I mean, if it's just words, I can tell them to mind their own business. If they keep going, I can say something Joshua said once to an irate worker, "Do you kiss your momma with that mouth?" However, if they won't go away and threaten us, I will defend you."

Carol took his hand back. "Okay, that's all I could ask of any man. Just so you know, there's a history with our family."

Bill nodded, "I wondered. I mean, your hair appears to be, you know."

Carol twisted a long strand around her finger and gazed into Bill's eyes. "You mean, it's not an afro."

Bill shrugged, "Well, I admit I don't know much about any races or genetics. Just what they taught at the orphanage and college, and I doubt most of those white professors knew anything beyond the campus boundaries.

"It isn't something I think about, honestly. I mean, I love your hair, but I'm in love with you, if that makes sense."

Carol kissed Bill's cheek, "That makes complete sense. That's part of the reason I love you. In so many ways, you're still just a boy trying to figure out the world and all you want is to find a family. I wish we were all that innocent.

"Unfortunately, for the rest of us, life has never been that simple. I need to warn you, my family's history may cause you some trouble the first time you meet my family. My great-grandmother married a white man. Although she came from a poor family, they had land. Once she married my great-grandfather the family disowned her. She had nothing except what she and her husband built.

"It took until my father's generation for them to become landowners again. Before that they were basically sharecroppers. There are some in my family that will see us together and fear history is repeating itself."

"Like your dad?"

Carol shook her head. "No, like my brother. Are you going to be okay putting up with that? I mean, my brother can be abrasive, and he defends me like you do. So, before we take the next step, you must gain his approval as well as my dad's. I don't want to live in a situation where I have to play referee between my brother and the man I love."

Bill finished off his beer and staired at the waves. "Well?" asked Carol.

Bill turned to Carol and leaned in until their lips almost touched. "For you, I will find a way to make it work, no matter what."

Her soft lips barely touched his, and she stood up. "Good, I need to head back to my room and get things packed up for heading home tomorrow. Think about all of this. It's only a few days before you meet my family."

Bill stood and held his breath as he watched her saunter out in her bikini. She lingered for a moment after opening the front door, and then disappeared. Bill realized he was holding his breath and exhaled. Bill looked up at the sky, "Any hints or ideas would be helpful."

Only the roar of the waves and the laughter and squeals of delight rose and fell across the wind. Somewhere in the back of Bill's mind a thought came forward. "Just be yourself." Bill stood still and wondered if any other thoughts would pop in his brain. After several seconds, he headed inside to start packing.

***

The odor of diesel filled Bill's nostrils as it wafted back from the exhaust pipe sticking out of the top of the old Ford skip loader. It was chilly by Wilson Mills, North Carolina standards, around forty-five degrees. Carol's father, Doug, and her brother, Evan, stood there with their arms crossed.

Bill waved and pointed to the disc harrow. He slid the gears into low third, lifted the bucket, and eased off the clutch. The tractor lurched forward and Bill feathered the foot pedal to steady the engine. After a few quick turns, he backed the tractor to the implement. Bill manhandled the three-point hitch this way and that to get it into the correct slots and secure it in place with cotter pins.

Doug walked around, reached in, and cut off the tractor.

Bill wrinkled his forehead, "Did I do something wrong?"

Evan said, "I didn't know rich white boys could handle a tractor."

Doug added, "Not to mention looking happy about the work. My daughter told me you're Wall Street."

Bill waited for Doug to walk back over to Evan and then answered. "When I was growing up at the orphanage, the groundskeeper, Mr. McCray, took me under his wing. I learned how to use tractors, lawnmowers, trimmers, anything to do with landscaping. I'm your man. We had a tractor just like yours that I worked with as a teenager."

Doug replied, "Ain't you full of surprises. I reckon you never mentioned your time at the orphanage to my daughter. I'm sure she would have told me if you had."

Bill cleared his throat. "Well, sir, it's a little hard to explain."

Evan interjected, "Why don't you try."

Bill rubbed the back of his neck, "Alright. Well, I only got most of my memories back over the last few months. I mean, I've never forgotten Mr. McCray. It's just, merging what I knew with my repressed memories took some time."

Evan shook his head. "I knew it. Carol's got herself mixed up with some crazy white boy. I told her to stay away, but she's one of these girls that don't see her hand in front of her face. She says it's all about the soul."

Doug turned to his son, "You mind what you say about your sister, boy. She's a godly woman, and you could learn some things from her." Doug turned back to Bill, "I'm aware of what you've been through. That ain't none of my business. I only want to know your intentions with my daughter."

Evan added, "And my sister."

His dad looked back at Evan and nodded once in approval.

Bill looked down and kicked a pebble at the toe of his boot. He sighed and looked Doug right in the eye. "Mr. Lewis, I wanted to have this conversation later, privately."

Doug answered, "I think it's best we do it now. I've got a busy weekend, and I'm liable to fall asleep before my butt hits the chair this evening."

Evan walked up and stood on his tiptoes until his nose almost touched Bill's. He snarled, "I want to know too. I'm not going to let some white boy disrespect my sister."

Bill looked into Evan's eyes that were almost reaching his. He thought about how similar they looked to his sister's.

Bill snarled back, "Good."

Evan took two steps back, and Bill continued, "I know you're protecting your sister. I want to protect her too. Carol means the world to me. Our friendship has grown over our time together, and I've come to realize I can't live without her. She understands me, knows how I think, sometimes she knows what I'm going to do before I do.

"I've always wanted a family, but I went about it the wrong way the first time. I tried to possess the woman I loved. I cornered her into becoming a family instead of giving us time and growing together. It wasn't that we didn't love each other. We did. Her death nearly destroyed me. But, Carol has helped me to understand that this is the better way, the way God intended.

"We understand each other. No, we aren't alike. That's part of what I love about her, but don't get me wrong, I'm not living in some fantasy. I understand we may have issues down the road, and our children may get picked on. I know there'll always be racists, but I don't let people like that decide how I'm going to live, and neither does your daughter."

Doug interjected, "It ain't just white people that are racists. Some of our relatives may quit talking to Carol, and maybe even the whole family if she marries you. You can expect some black folks to be less than kind to your kids, depending on how they come out."

Bill replied, "Carol told me that. We both know we'll have to work hard for our family." He took a deep breath and squared his shoulders. "It doesn't make any difference, though. She and I love each other. I'm not saying love solves every problem, but I will do everything in my power to make sure she knows she is wanted and loved."

Evan reached down, picked up a rock, threw it, and then said, "Dang. I ain't ever loved a girl that much. If you mean it. But if you don't." Evan quickly snatched up another rock, and it ricocheted off Bill's boot.

Doug pointed at the disc harrow, "Have a seat."

Bill backed up and eased down onto a cold metal bar.

Doug put his boot up on the bar next to Bill and stood over him.

He said, "Alright, I'm convinced you're sincere, and I know you can protect my daughter from what she's told me.

"Now, I want to talk to you man to man for a minute. What's your game plan for when you hurt her, or she hurts you?"

Bill's eyes narrowed, and he glared at Doug. "I'd never hurt her."

Doug dropped his leg and sat next to Bill. "Uh-huh. That's what we all say. I've been married to the same woman for forty years. I quit counting the times we've gotten mad at each other. Although my wife could probably give you the number."

Doug snickered at his own joke and continued, "Listen to me and listen good. Young people all think they're different from the older generation. The truth is, we're all repeating the same mistakes over and over again. So, I want to give you some free advice, and I suggest you take it for more than it's worth.

"When you fight, and you will fight, watch what you say. When the person you love disappoints you or makes you angry, you'll tend to want to lash out verbally. Before you do, stop and ask yourself if it's worth it. If Carol says something that hurts you, are you going to take it or give back as good as you got?"

Bill pursed his lips for a few seconds before answering. "I don't know. I can't imagine ever getting that mad at Carol."

Doug replied, "Well, imagine it or not, it's going to happen. So, let me make this easy for you. You can argue with my daughter, yell at her, and even make her cry. However, if you ever demean her, if you make her feel like she's less of a woman than she is, you and I will have words. And if you ever lift a finger against her, I'll kill you."

Evan walked up until his feet touched Bill's. He said, "That goes double for me."

Bill nodded, "Message received."

Evan backed up.

Doug asked, "So, do you still want to marry my daughter and be a part of this family?"

Bill stood, dusted off his hind end, smacked his hands together to make sure they were clean, stuck his hand out to Doug, and said, "If you'll have me."

Doug shook Bill's hand, "Welcome to the family."

Evan walked over and stuck out his hand, "I sure hope my sister is right about you."

Bill smiled, "Me too."

Doug invited Bill to disc a five-acre field so he and Evan could take care of some maintenance in the shop. Bill was ecstatic. He spent the next couple of hours thinking back to the happy memories with Mr. McCray. The sun was seated just above the tree line when he pulled up to the outbuildings near the maintenance shop. Carol came out with a cup of hot chocolate, and Doug joined her.

Bill slid off the tractor, and Carol handed the warm cup to Bill. It was a welcome change from the cold breeze on the tractor.

Carol kissed Bill on the cheek and then said, "I was just telling Daddy that you may be taking a job in California."

Bill felt the blood leave his face. He turned to Doug, "Um, sir, I don't know if I'm taking it. What I mean is, I wasn't trying to hide that from you or anything earlier."

Doug snickered and then laughed. When he had calmed down, he said, "Boy, you need to learn to relax. It doesn't matter where you live. I'll know how to find you if I need to."

Bill said, "Yes, sir."

Doug winked at Bill, gave his daughter a peck on the cheek, and went back inside the shop.

Carol slid her arm under Bill's and snuggled against him. "It looks like you won over Daddy."

Bill let out a sigh. He said, "Your dad scares me more than Chuck."

Carol turned Bill to her and slammed her lips against his. Bill's head went light, energy pulsed through his body, and he pulled Carol in tighter. They finally let go of one another.

Carol smiled, poked Bill in the chest, and said, "Good. Daddy is much scarier than Chuck could ever hope to be. So, stay on his good side, and everything will be alright."

Carol strolled back towards the farmhouse and gave him a finger wave over her shoulder.

Bill looked up at the sky, "Thank you."

***

Carol wrapped her arms around Bill's waist and pressed her body against his back. "I still can't believe we're living in Malibu."

Bill attempted to comb through his wavy locks and miss his wife's head. He gave up on his hair and reached back and held his wife. After a few moments, she stepped back, moved over to her sink, and began to touch up her makeup.

"You know, your brother's place still intimidates me."

Bill glanced over at her in the mirror. "Intimidates you? How do you figure?"

"He has servants."

Bill rolled his eyes. "Please, he has a big house. Besides, he sponsored the family. They were stuck at the border. Now they have an income, a place to live, and their child is in school. Who knows what would've happened with the pandemic and everything."

Carol turned to Bill. "I know. I'm not saying it's a bad thing. It's just, well, this is the sort of thing I fought against in college. You know, the one percent, but Harold has me all twisted up. He's got all this money, but he shares it with his workers at the company and at home. He wants people to succeed, to be happy. That just isn't how I pictured the wealthy."

Bill asked, "What did you think they were like?"

Carol finished her lips and tossed her makeup back in the sink drawer. "You know, grumpy white guys. Like the guys you see on your finance cable channels."

"Well, those guys exist purely for the cash. Harold sees money as a tool, not an end. He wants to make his part of the world better."

Carol asked, "Are there others like him?"

Bill turned and slipped his arms around Carol. "There's good and bad everywhere, honey."

She ran the tip of her fingernail down the bridge of his nose. "Well, you treat me good, and I'll be bad for you later."

Bill shivered.

Carol turned to leave, "Good boy."

The two made their way from their hillside home above Harold's estate. They walked across the small two-lane road, and through the arched entryway to Harold's front door. The California sun shown brightly on the front of the Spanish estate. Bill reached over and rang the doorbell.

Harold hollered from somewhere inside, "I've got that."

The sound of heavy footsteps jogging grew louder. They stopped just on the other side of the door, but nothing happened for a moment. Bill looked over at Carol, smiled, and hit the doorbell again.

The door flew open.

Harold said, "Billy, Carol, you two look lovely. Please come in."

Bill replied, "Harry. I hope you aren't too out of breath on our account."

Harold slapped Bill's back, "I could use the exercise."

They followed Harold out of the foyer, through the living room, and out to the patio. The grill was smoking, and Harold rushed over, lifted the lid, and flipped the rows of burgers attempting to burn.

The door opened behind them, and Darla and Sofia came out. Darla pointed Sofia to Bill and Carol. She handed each of them a beer.

"Thank you," said Carol.

"Yes, thank you," responded Bill.

"It is my pleasure."

Darla pointed at the round table where place settings had already been arranged. "Harold, you, Bill, and Carol need to have a seat. Sofia, please finish making lunch."

Harold and Bill looked at each other, and then Carol. Bill looked back at Darla and noticed a manila envelope she had managed to keep partially hidden next to her khaki shorts. Harold sat, Bill and Carol did the same.

Darla held up the envelope. "Garcia sent this to me. It's information about your mother."

Bill asked, "What sort of information?"

Darla extended the envelope to Bill, "Take a look."

Harold asked, "How long have you had that?"

Darla answered, "Garcia called and told me I had a package for you and Bill. I picked it up at my P.O. Box today."

"Why do you think I'd want it?" asked Harold.

"I'm just the messenger."

Bill spoke up, "Harry, what do you want to do. Read it, or burn it?"

"Let's read it, and then maybe we'll burn it."

Bill nodded as he tore open the envelope and pulled out the piece of paper.

Harold asked, "Well, what does it say?"

Bill looked up, "Sorry.

"Basically, it's a list of aliases she went by. Let's see, April, Star, Silver, and Alice."

"Alice," said Harold.

Bill and Harold looked up at Darla.

She said, "Don't look at me. I wasn't involved in any of this."

Harold asked, "Is our mom CIA?"

Darla answered, "If she's with the agency, I've never met her. Bill, you said those are aliases. Does it list her real name?"

Bill glanced over the sheet of paper, "Rachael Bell."

Darla said, "Never heard of her."

Harold asked, "Bill, is there anything else?"

Bill nodded, "Some places she lived. Let's see, northern California, and then Alabama, but it ends there."

"Did she die?" asked Carol.

Bill shook his head, "It doesn't say anything. It just ends there. Oh, and I have your real name, Harry."

Harold bristled, "Harold is my real name."

"Your born name. The name they changed."

Darla asked, "What is it?"

"Thomas Bell."

Harold started to laugh. Bill cocked his head, "What's so funny?"

Darla answered while Harold got control of himself, "You've met his best friend, Tom."

Harold spoke up, "Yea, I was just picturing the look on his face if he knew I was Tom too."

Bill flipped the page over. It was blank.

Harold asked, "That's it?"

Bill nodded, "Looks like it. That was a big build-up to nothing."

Harold turned to Darla, "Why did Garcia send this? He always has a reason."

"He didn't share it with me. Maybe he wanted you boys to understand a little more about your mother. I'm guessing she was in California, so she could be closer to you when you were having problems. She probably moved back towards the south in hopes of reuniting with Bill one day."

Bill tossed the paper on the table, "Possibly. Well, if she's still alive, I wish her the best."

Harold added, "So do I. I hope life was kinder to her than it was to Hunter."

Bill grabbed his beer bottle and tilted it towards Harold, "I'll drink to that."

Bill took a swallow and then put the bottle back down. "Now, what about that food?"

Carol spoke up, "Wait. You mean you're going to drop it just like that? Doesn't your mother mean anything to you?"

Bill answered, "Sure, but that's in the past. I didn't really know her. Harold's real mother passed away. We both appreciate what April, or Rachael, or whatever she went by, did for us. But if I've learned anything lately, it's that we can't dwell in the past."

Bill reached over and took Carol's hand. Then he grabbed Harold's as well. "This is our family now. I don't know what the future holds, but we need to push forward with the path God's given us, and I'm thankful to be on the journey with all of you."

Bill dropped his grip, and Carol leaned over, wrapped her arms around Bill, and said, "To our family."

She gave Bill a lengthy kiss. His world lit up, and his head felt light. The warm California sun sparkled brightly off of the unending ocean. The smell of meat beginning to burn wafted across his nostrils, and Harold jumped up and ran to the grill.

New Mexico

Rachael pushed open the worn screen door on her faded gray double-wide. The afternoon winds had started to move east across the plateau in Torrance County. She stepped down into the fenced backyard and began to throw out the chickens' daily ration of food.

"Here chick, chick, chick,"

The biddies moved in mass towards the feed that was being spread before Rachael's feet. The back door to the trailer creaked opened, and Rachael reached inside her can, grabbed a pistol, and brought it to bear as she turned on her heel and allowed the can and feed to spill to the ground.

"Oh, Preacher Man. You can get yourself killed sneaking up on me." Exclaimed Rachael as an audible sigh escaped behind her words.

"Preacher Man. I haven't heard that from you in a long time. I tried knocking, but nobody answered."

"What brings you to the middle of nowhere? I hope you haven't lost the faith."

The man adjusted the cowboy hat that he was clearly not comfortable wearing. "You know me better than that, Alice. My faith is what keeps me in this nasty business."

"I've told you before, call me by my name."

The man mumbled, "This is official business."

Rachael's neatly trimmed eyebrows rose, "Since when are we official business?"

She turned back to the chickens gorging themselves. Rachael fought to retrieve some of the feed and dropped the gun back into the can with a clang. She spoke loudly to the man behind her. "And take off those sunglasses. I've missed looking into your eyes."

"Yes, ma'am." The man said as he reached up and removed his sunglasses. "It's been a long time."

Rachael turned to face him. "This was your idea, remember? Stay away from the boys. Stay apart until the danger passed. How many years have I waited?"

"Too many."

Rachael bumped past him and made her way back inside her mobile home. The dust from the afternoon winds had penetrated the screened doors and windows and created a soft tan haze throughout the house. Rachael sat down on her couch and pointed at the other end of the sofa. He complied.

Rachael took off her straw hat, and thick flowing raven locks fell below her shoulders.

The man smiled and said, "My God, I've missed seeing your beautiful hair and looking into your sparkling blue eyes."

Rachael smiled, and the two sat there staring at each other without saying a word. It felt like several minutes had passed before she spoke.

"Garcia."

"Yes."

"Are we just going to sit here like we just met?"

Garcia sighed, "Business before pleasure, my bride. I need to give you my debrief."

Rachael nodded, "Did Bill ever ask about me?"

"He only wants to know why you left him a prisoner in the orphanage. Harold wants to know if you're still alive, but only for Bill's sake."

"Did you send Darla the envelope?"

Garcia nodded.

"Did Darla tell you what they said?"

Garcia cleared his throat. "I'm not sure you'll like this. They toasted to your memory. Both of the boys have moved on after that ugly business and are focusing on the future."

A tear trickled down Rachael's cheek. "It's for the best, at least for now."

"Why?" asked Garcia.

"They're not ready. I'm not ready."

Garcia responded, "The longer you wait, the less ready you'll be. I know I pushed you to stay away from the boys, but that time has passed. Hunter's dead, and his terrorist cells splintered. They aren't in any danger."

Rachael stood up and started to pace. "Don't you see? They don't need me."

Garcia stood, wrapped his arms around her waist, and held her tight, "But I need you, and I need our son."

Rachael smiled at him, and she could swear their bodies were tingling together. She pushed back from him and said, "There it is. You want to tell Bill. What do you think he'll do when he finds out the man involved in bringing death and destruction to his life is actually his dad?"

Garcia protested, "You can't lay that on me. That was all Chuck. I protected our son."

Rachael walked up, gave Garcia a gentle kiss on the cheek, and spoke softly. "I know that, but how do you think Bill will see it, or Harold for that matter? The agent sent to protect his family is actually his stepfather?"

Garcia answered, "That's not how Harold thinks. Richard and Barbara were his parents, full stop. So, what are you saying? We have to hide and lie to the boys the rest of our lives?"

Rachael moved back to the couch and pointed Garcia to the spot beside her. He complied. She said, "Look, you're the one who recruited me into the agency. You told me at the time that I would have to make a lot of personal sacrifices, and it was worth it to me to stop Hunter.

"I'm not saying we can never tell the boys I'm alive."

Garcia's face grew tight. "Bill needs to know his heritage. He isn't just a Berserker. The blood of Aztec super warriors runs in his veins. He is a Shorn One, just like my ancestors. Bill needs training like Harold. Counseling can only do so much without discipline."

Rachael answered, "I'm just saying that now isn't the time.

"Bill just started his new family. Harold finally has his company in some semblance of order. Darla has been rewarded with watching her own family stateside while she gets some downtime. I'm not going to interfere in any of that. We'll tell them but give our boys time to breathe."

Garcia's shoulders slumped, "You're right, as usual."

Rachael smiled, "That's why I'm the boss at home and at work."

Garcia raised his index finger, "About that. With Alice's passing, I've been promoted. We're peers now."

Rachael's eyes widened, "I see. Well, don't let that give you any ideas."

Garcia leaned into her body, "What kind of ideas."

Rachael's eyes sparkled, "I know we've been apart too long, but I didn't' say we were through talking."

Garcia began to push her backward with his body. Rachael shoved him off the couch, and he landed on his back on the floor. She leaped and straddled his body while she pinned down his arms. "Did I say the meeting was adjourned?"

Garcia bucked and rolled her off him and got on top of her. "No, I did."

Rachael wrapped her legs around his waist and squeezed. Garcia winced, gasped, and collapsed to the floor when Rachael released him. She straddled his body once more. "It's adjourned when I say so."

She dove down and kissed Garcia hard. He could taste blood and wondered whose lip was cut. She sat up, "Now it's adjourned."

www.ingramcontent.com/pod-product-compliance
Lightning Source LLC
Chambersburg PA
CBHW021307190726
48288CB00003B/728